THE STAR CAFÉ

THE STAR CAFÉ

& Other Stories

MARY CAPONEGRO

CHARLES SCRIBNER'S SONS
New York

Charles Scribner's Sons
Macmillan Publishing Company
866 Third Avenue, New York, NY 10022
Collier Macmillan Canada, Inc.

Library of Congress Cataloging-in-Publication Data
Caponegro, Mary, 1956–
  The Star Café & other Stories / Mary Caponegro.
    p. cm.
  Contents: Tales from the next village—The Star Café—Materia prima—Sebastian.
  ISBN 0–684–19113–X
  I. Title.
PS3553.A5877S74 1990
813'.54—dc20   90–8209   CIP

The following stories appeared in somewhat different form in: *Conjunctions 7*, "Tales from the Next Village" copyright © 1985; *Mississippi Review 34/35*, "The Star Café" copyright © 1984; *Conjunctions 10*, "Materia Prima" copyright © 1987.

All of the above, with the exception of "Materia Prima," also appeared in the small-press volume *Tales From the Next Village*, published by Lost Roads Press in 1985.

The author gratefully acknowledges permission to reprint excerpts from: *The I Ching or Book of Changes*, the Richard Wilhelm translation rendered into English by Cary F. Baynes, Bollingen Series #19, copyright © 1950, 1967, 1977 by Princeton University Press; "Birds as Flying Machines" by Carl Welty, copyright © 1955, and "How Birds Sing" by Crawford H. Greenwalt, copyright © 1969, both from *Scientific American, Inc.*, all rights reserved; *A New Dictionary of Birds* edited by Sir A. Landsborough Thomson, copyright © 1964 by British Ornithologists' Union, published by McGraw-Hill Book Company; and *The Basic Works of Aristotle*, edited by Richard McKeon, copyright © 1941 by Oxford University Press, published by Random House, Inc.

10 9 8 7 6 5 4 3 2 1

Printed in the United States of America

for my mother and father

Contents

TALES FROM
THE NEXT VILLAGE

THIS CIRCULAR GARLAND IS AS VISible, as subtle, as a ring around a planet, but you must develop the telescope within yourself, your own inner eye, to see the beauty of the chain it makes, its variegated texture of feather, skin, fur, slimy or smooth, wrapped tight to turn the earth with a motion too slow to measure on your most sophisticated instrument, not even eternity's second hand.

If it isn't the year of the rooster it must be the year of the pig. Is it the dog? The fish? Use the process of elimination; check the list of endangered species, since each year annihilates what came before: tiger eats wolf, wolf eats monkey, infant eats parent, and alchemy takes the entrails. If you cultivate a special sight, you can see that circular succession, as defined as a constellation.

It is common knowledge that at the end another sort of ark will come, this one with wings and cockpit. It will let down its tiny stairs; and only then that complex chain will relinquish its hold. Each link will slough itself off and up each step, never in pairs, but singly, until the last animal boards, commemorating this final new year: the year of the serpent, who eats its skin as the earth's last act. You find you are squeamish; we are all made squeamish by the end of the world, never again by water.

If only you had the training to see the beauty of it: being rid of all that oldness. And then the stairs contract into the sky: the winged ark flies straight into the sun. There is no more.

3

I

He says he has to sit under a tree to think something over, but Chiao-hisao is going to the sea, because he remembers the song his mother used to sing about the silk the mermaids sell. If it's true, that's a truth that interests him; that's the one he wants to go out seeking, even though he feels guilty because he knows he should be an internal explorer.

Guilt dissolves all too rapidly when he hears their voices, singing the same song his mother used to. He is entranced by their lovely, subtle dissonances and their silver scales, glistening in the moonlight: the sleek suits of these women wrapped in fish.

"May I buy?" Chiao calls to them, and becomes still bolder, tries playfully to catch them by their tail fins as they swim by, teasing, just out of reach. He wades in the water to be one with them, but they won't open where he wants them; they lead him deeper. He reaches out frantically and makes contact with a fish-part, but she's so slippery he can't keep hold.

They go deeper still, and now it's no game; he's trying to hold on for dear life, the water well over his head. He can't even grasp; his hand just glides, over this silk that is suddenly sub-stanceless texture.

He wonders if they have the power to contract their bodies like tortoises. He wonders if he is drowning now. He wishes he could hold onto something.

"Where's the rest of you?" he shouts, over and over into the din of the waves, his tone changing by stages from commanding to pleading. The sounds he hears form no articulated answer. Their liquid voices.

II

Pi Tz'u and Hsiang 'Ai, man and wife, loved as much as mortals can, but what flowed from him to her in love made her allergic.

All the village's sympathy was not consolation, but love was. Love was something of a consolation.

When Pi Tz'u died of natural causes, the village sighed, that quality of sigh one hears when the ill or elderly are mercifully taken, that breathy sound that serves also as a clearing of the throat to open the way for gossip.

"At last," they said, "Hsiang 'Ai is free to find another, a love without side effects, an untainted bliss," though there were those who argued the pattern would repeat. They said this with the same breath in which they talked about the weather. And with every storm, they reminded each other that Pi Tz'u's spirit was mixed with all the other spirits that rained upon the earth.

"What mortals do for love," they said to each other, clicking their tongues, remembering the couple's sacrifice, and then someone would speculate about whether acupuncture would have helped, and then there would be silence for a while.

The village children, certain that there were more wondrous things in this world than talk, were always seeking diversion, often getting into mischief in the process. During storms they were particularly restless. They preferred the rain to their parents' chatter, and left, but didn't dare disclose to their elders what they had stumbled upon, what so compelled them that they repeated the pilgrimage during every storm thereafter. They would have been severely scolded, perhaps even beaten if they had reported what they saw: Hsiang 'Ai in the sodden field, her thighs splayed like butterfly wings, white wings gently opening and closing while the rose that hinged them blinked in the rain.

III

Hsing-chê hangs upside down from a tree, seeking the cinnabar fields and the breath within. He tries to focus only upon that breath, not the seeking. Hsing feels closer and closer to oneness, until he becomes aware of the semen collecting in his head, dripping with the slow regularity of a leak from one of the bamboo pipes that lead to the cistern, or perhaps more like the drops shed by a leaf after rain, from its own more delicate, transient storage. This one moment of distraction is enough to disrupt his meditation; he loses whatever balance he had thus far achieved, and falls to the ground.

Six peasant girls who have stopped to rest on their way back from fetching a more ordinary water see the fate of this might-have-been-enlightened one. Aware of the store of fertility in the head of this detoured bodhi, they waste neither time nor propriety in sucking out all the nourishment contained therein, as avid as thieves to a dead man's wallet. Instinctively, each puts her own mouth to a sense organ: ear, nostril or eye, and there is a fight over who will have access to the mouth.

For three nights and four days they sustain this intimate vigil. On the fourth day, with numb jaws and aching muscles, they cease. There is no life left in him. Hsing's body resembles a piece of wrinkled parchment, or a balloon after all the air has seeped out. Possessed with the new strength of his transferred vital force, the six of them lift him, one at his feet, two at each side, and the last, the one who sucked from his mouth, cradles his head. With the delicacy and purposefulness of a committee chosen to hang the largest and most valuable ornament on a festival tree, they replace him in his original position.

That is why, to this day, we do not pick the leaves from the trees, and when autumn makes them fall, we gather them reverently into baskets before burning.

IV

Without any explanation, and as far as he knew, preparation, she walked out and tied herself to a tree, a yew-tree, one of the garden's loveliest. He went out later that afternoon, having noticed her absence, and scolded her: "Up to your old tricks, Yu-

Hsing, I know you're just doing it for attention. Untie yourself immediately."

You wouldn't think a binding done by one's own hand would be so stubborn, he didn't think, but what he didn't realize was, that all the time she'd spent ostensibly studying flower arranging, she'd actually been engaged in learning the language of knots. She knew every kind, and how to make a fortress of their secrets.

Thus he made no progress with his thick fingers. They were no match for the skillfully fashioned rope-blossoms, or the majestic splint to which her body was affixed. He retreated to his solitary abode, and every morning from then on, his bed was damp with the sweat of nightmares and his yearning.

But as he dreamt dark forests, she said mantras, chanted to her tree, "O noble yew, I bind to you to make myself strong, let me become your firm-rooted, enduring majesty." But even in her strength she sometimes thirsted for the earth's fruits or his seed, recalling ancient tenderness.

There were days she almost weakened when he called to her, in a voice less and less reproachful, more and more entreating, once even seeking her forgiveness rather than her repentance. "Before you are unreachable," he'd said, for even now the texture of her once-smooth flesh was changing, coarsening.

At times Yu-Hsing wanted to call out to him or somehow comfort him, but she knew all her work would then be lost, and he might not even recognize her woody voice.

After the seventh day he no longer slept, but paced outside the door, and on the eighth night he kept vigil to the process, right beside her, as one attends the loved one's death bed, to know the exact moment of transition.

At dawn, the village made a circle around the yew-tree, too late to have seen his fervent tongue at the smooth white bark all night, but there to know what day's first light revealed, a thing they'd never seen of any sort of tree: not a lightning-made fissure, but a flexing of that solid trunk, and his limbs wrapped around its body, his own trunk in the grasp of so many branches.

V

Wu-nêng comes back from market with pigeon and horse-flesh. Only one place stocks the forbidden foods; only there can one buy the black fish that come from the jade river. The week's earnings were spent on this one meal: a stew of all the forbidden meats and viands: horse, dog, bullock, goose, pigeon, leeks, garlic, onions, scallions—his own private recipe. Wu's breath will reek from this gluttony, but he's certain it won't matter where he's going: the back road to immortality. Impatient with enlightenment; he wants something tangible, something to hold onto.

He lays the ingredients on the table, making piles of the neatly cut pieces. In the center is a special pile of fins, eyes, tails and hair, to be added last. Tears come as he slices the green and white vegetables, but that's just a tiny trial; those tears will be more than compensated for.

The fire is going strongly now. He stirs each item in turn, until everything is melded, thick with brownish sauce. This feast will surely be succulent. Now he knows a well-kept secret: that knowledge of forbidden fruits is available to those who take the risk; and if knowledge is exile he doesn't care. He's bored with bliss, and besides he never felt comfortable sitting in that unnatural position.

He takes an implement to serve himself the feast from his finest dish, his grandmother's gold tureen. She would not approve, but she need never know. Wu is glad to have the meal all to himself, obliged to share his delicious concoction with no one.

The first bite that he had anticipated savoring is the foulest taste he has ever encountered. But after such trouble and expense, he is determined to ingest the whole of his self-inflicted prescription.

Immediately after, he lies down, feeling too weak to cleanse

8

the vessels. Only as an afterthought does he disrobe, because the air is so close in the room that he can't sleep; feels he can barely breathe. Seeking fresher air, Wu goes outside; lies down beside an oak tree. Although belches plague him all night, the coolness is relief. Sleep finally comes.

The next morning, he wakes, still feeling nauseous, unable to rid himself of the horrible after-taste. He rises and sees the view of the village he has always seen from his house, but a reduced version, as if from a great distance. Rubbing his eyes fails to improve their focus; the village still looks much farther away than he knows it actually is.

Thus exposed in the morning light, Wu-nêng remembers his nakedness. In the distance he sees someone coming toward him; it is a woman. She too is naked. Wu is embarrassed by his own bareness, but cannot help delighting in hers as she approaches. He holds out his hand, and to his further delight, she stretches out hers.

The space between them is bridged; they touch for a moment. She explodes. He is horrified, though this event is accompanied by neither blood nor noise. Instantly, silently, abstractly, she is dismembered and gone from him, until he looks back at his farsighted view of the village, and recognizes the many tiny versions of her, running in every direction, inaccessible to him.

VI

Her grandmother says, "When a woman of wealth accepts the hand of a poor man, it does not bode well for the marriage."

"But love, ancestor," Fan Tui T'a protests, "what of love, whose flaming sword lays waste any obstacle, whose army stands always prepared for victorious battle; love, who is all vanquishing and cannot be vanquished, love who has no mercy?"

"O child," grandmother scolds, "you know so little of the world. You dream more than think. I tell you it is a mistake to marry beneath you."

Every night thereafter, Fan Tui T'a recites the private vows
she has formulated:

I will give up my gorgeous robes
I will give up my tortoise combs.
I will give up exotic flowers
and pick instead the daisies.
The curtains between rooms will be
of plain cloth, the screens
unadorned. I shall not mourn
the riches of my past life.

This becomes her mantra; it is with her throughout the
wedding ceremony, chanted silently, as she makes a mental fire
with all the lovely articles inside it. Yet they resist the flame. As
she renounces each thing by word, it is all the more brightly
illuminated in her mind. But tonight, Fan thinks, there will be no
room for images to interfere.

After the simple ceremony, they lie in his cold hut on the
straw mat that is not quite wide enough or long enough. There
is no servant to bring them tea. She closes her eyes, and thinks
how little different it is to have them open, in this dark, barren
interior, such a contrast to the ornately furnished surroundings
she is used to. She misses the gold and jade objects, the scrolls
on the walls, the evidences of her achievements in embroidery
and calligraphy. She might have had a vast, scarlet-painted wedding bed, in a curtained-off portico the size of the whole hut,
with figures of the great and virtuous ones painted on its golden
panels.

Here there is nothing but darkness and flesh and the smell
of damp earth. No fragrance of flowers. As he begins to caress
her, Fan Tui T'a imagines her former servants removing jewelry
from her neck and wrists to place in the velvet-lined drawers of
the tall, gold-inlaid chest; she remembers how it felt to stroke
the velvet with her finger. As she touches her hair, she sees the

servants skillfully coiling it for her in the morning, sometimes ornamenting it with flowers, undoing it in the evening. As she feels his weight against her, she remembers being carried here in the scarlet wedding chair. She will never again see anything as fine as that, never again be attended on in that fashion.

Now her arms and feet rub lightly against the earthen floor, and the final image preceding sleep is that of the servants assisting her manicure, rubbing a pumice stone against her heels and elbows, the only sites on her body where the skin has even a hint of roughness.

In dream, Fan Tui T'a journeys through the house she no longer inhabits. She goes over the spirit wall, through the great gate, past the gatekeeper's room, the reception hall and covered passageway, the courtyard, heaven's well, the back court, the flower-wall and servants' lower house.

She dwells a while with the buddha images in the two-story apartments, then goes through the side-inner apartment: the place for poor relations, where she might have resided with him. Then through the eastern flower hall, the entertainment hall, empty now; the male servants' lower house, the great book room, in which she also lingers; the western flower hall, where the fragrance is almost overpowering. When Fan comes to the boudoir, with its excellent light, where she has spent so much time painting, writing and embroidering, she cannot bear to stay. She goes through the kitchen, has difficulty negotiating the passage of many turnings, as if the spirits were making it hard for her, or as if the passage regarded her as a bad spirit.

Once through, there is only the study and pavilion remaining until she arrives at the furthest point: the stable. There is one horse there, lying on straw on the ground. She has never seen a horse lying down before. Can something be the matter with it? She walks cautiously over and bends down next to it, strokes gingerly its sleek nose and neck and matted mane. Its eye seems very large.

At this points Fan Tui T'a wakes. But her environment has

not changed. She screams to realize her surroundings have not altered between dream and waking. Something is stepping on her hand and almost suffocating her. There is hair in her mouth. Large prominent nostrils and a long, u-shaped row of teeth press against her small, delicate mouth, as she is gazed upon by an immense brown eye. The creature is so close to her that she can barely see it. "You must have had a bad dream," it is saying. "Let me hold you."

VII

"Nine in the fourth place means: no game in the field."

For days Heng Hsin hunted pheasant in the wood, without success. He thought he might go mad if he didn't shoot one soon. He felt like screaming.

Three times a day, Mi Huo came to the wood where Heng Hsin paced with his weapon.

"I have prepared a meal for you, Hsin," she would say. "Won't you rest your gun on the ground and partake?"

"Please, Huo," he would reply, annoyed, "you know I cannot rest until I've shot one. But how can that happen with your constant interruptions? Every time you intrude, you scare them away, that might have been about to venture forth from behind a tree."

"And if no pheasant should appear, Hsin? What then? You know what it says in the book: 'A man who persists in stalking game in a place where there is none may wait forever without finding any.'"

"Don't curse my chances. Perseverance will lead to success."

"But Hsin, don't you remember what we learned when we had the coins thrown?—'Six in the fifth place means, giving duration to one's character through perseverance. This is good fortune for a woman, misfortune for a man.'"

"Do you want me to fail, Huo? You might be more encouraging. You might trust me. I am only trying to provide for you. If you would wait at home, I would soon be there with the food for dinner."

"But Hsin, I don't care about that; I only want you. You don't need to be the hunter and provider. It is what the book says that counts: 'A woman should follow a man her whole life long, but a man should at all times hold to what is his duty at the given moment.' You see, I am only being obedient; while you, you must admit, are being stubborn."

"Go home, woman. I have my own sense of honor, which you cannot begin to understand. This is what I must hold to for this moment."

"And the next, and the next and next, I suppose," she muttered as she turned to take her leave. "Starve then, for all I care."

For years she waited in the house.

One day she heard a knock at the door. She knew it was he, though there was no way she could have known. And a lucky thing, because she might not have recognized him, so changed was his appearance. As mine must also be, she thought.

"I see you have finally come to your senses, old man, and are ready to admit your folly. You have come to ask my forgiveness for all that wasted time."

"On the contrary, old woman, I bring not contrition, but blame. It is your fault I come so late and empty handed."

"You blame me, Hsin, you who never honored the moment, or a loving wife's desires. How many things we might have seen and done together while you stayed forever pacing with your heavy gun. The house is still, the bed is cold, the sun set every day on unfulfilled time. . . ."

"Do not continue. I will hear no more of this. We shall not waste what little is left of our lives. We must forget this wretched past. Tell me instead, what is it you carry in your hand, that is also spilled before the closet door; it looks like sand, or grain."

"Yes, it is sand, Hsin. You were away so long, the hourglass finally burst. I turned it constantly, thinking, he will come now, in an hour, in another hour."

"And what is that scratching noise? That is something new. Where does it come from?"

"I began to go mad with waiting, and now I scratch whatever comes to hand: my scalp, my skin, the walls."

"But what are these—feathers—on the floor? It is not like you to be so untidy with the housework."

"On the contrary, Hsin, I cleaned so much in your absence, to distract my sorrowful mind and heart, that I destroyed the dustmop, and now pieces of it are scattered throughout the house."

"I hear squawking, Huo; it comes from nearby. Can you explain this?"

"Poor old man, when one wants to hear something so badly, for so long, he may begin to imagine it. You need rest. Come lie down and I will help you forget. We will forgive each other all."

"No, that is the wrong door, Hsin; the bedroom is the other way. Don't you remember where the closet was; what could you want in the closet? There is nothing that concerns you there. I forbid you to open that door; I will not forgive you, Hsin . . ."

Behind the door he saw the renovated closet, and heard the sound, not imaginary, now amplified to an almost deafening pitch. He saw rows and rows of plump, feathered bodies, packed together like hats, or shoes. And staring at him, all those beaks and eyes.

VIII

Poor Teng Hou. Nothing will go right for him. He is lonely when he goes home at night, and frustrated when he works in the field with the older men during the day.

"What kind of life is this?" he complains to them. "I can't even keep my horse attached to my wagon."

"It's not so bad," one replies. "Look on the bright side."

"You exaggerate your difficulties," says another.

"What you need, Teng Hou," says a wise third, "is a wife."
Teng, upon reflection, agrees, and every day from then on,
he journeys to the north side of the village. There dwells the
maiden to whom he has secretly given his heart. The journey is
long and his courage is small, so in order to distract himself he
concentrates on the images that mark his path.

1) the fields with their top layer of new green shoots
2) men gathering mulberry leaves for the silkworms
3) women hatching the worms inside their coats
4) women washing clothes in the stream
5) women gathering plum blossoms on the banks of the
   stream
6) women stitching the blossoms into cloth
7) a flock of cranes
8) a boy drawing water from a well
9) servants bringing the traditional geese and silks to some
   bride's family
10) men and women together in the rice fields, planting

These same images, in reverse sequence, console him as he
returns, daily, with her refusal. The next morning he always makes
his report to the men who plow with him: "The maiden is chaste;
she will not pledge herself." They console him, persuade him to
try again when the plowing is done for the day: "Just keep trying,
Hou. This way she'll know you're serious."

This advice Teng also takes. In fact he is so assiduous in his
ardor that he makes the ritual of his pilgrimage through every
single season, from "the rains," "insects awaken," "vernal equinox,"
and "summer solstice," through "slight heat," "great heat," and
"stopping of heat," from "autumnal equinox," "hoar frost falls" and
"winter solstice," through "slight cold" and "great cold," until he
has come full circle as spring begins. He charts the complete cycle
many times, until those who had been most encouraging and
persuasive became skeptical, saying, amongst themselves, "Trust

Teng Hou to choose the most resolute virgin in the village," and to his face, "Hou, there are many blossoms in the garden, many fish in the ocean; how many harvests can you wait?"

For it had been nearly ten years.

"I will go one last time," Teng resolves, "then give up." On his last journey he particularly cherishes the sequence of images, as one might dwell upon the sight of snow one knows will shortly melt. What will her days be like, he wonders, without his visit, his question? Has she come in any way to depend upon it, as he has, regardless of the answer? Will she be relieved or regretful to realize he'll come no more? So weary and sorrowful is Teng by the time he arrives that he cannot even gaze at her as he asks the final time, turning away even before the sound has emerged from her lips, then toward her again, startled, unable to believe that he has heard, "Yes, I will pledge myself."

And neither can the ears of the earth believe.

The men, bent in a row over the fields of new green shoots, turn their heads, all at once, toward the sound. A symphony of women open their coats in a single gesture, as if they held a single banner. The boy holds his bucket suspended over the well as the women let all the wash float down the stream. Geese and silks, being carried to brides' families throughout the land, are let loose, making banners between the clouds. All is in motion, all is in flight, plum blossoms scattered over the gardens with half-finished embroidery lain aside, so that those who stitched could hear the sound, then see the sight, of the sun and moon colliding.

IX

Into the house she comes: my younger sister. As soon as I see them at the entrance she with her eyes demurely to the ground, he looking into my eyes for acceptance, I know, instantly, what I am to call her.

She is lovely, her high cheekbones like elegantly carved

ivory, her eyes like dark slivers of moon, her hair a dark, waveless lake. Exquisite tiny feet and hands.

My husband introduces her by name: "This is Kuei Mei."

"My sister," I greet her, kissing the promontory of her forehead as the landscape of her face shifts, bows.

Later, she assists me with the preparations for the evening meal. I call him from the other room.

"Why don't you take Kuei Mei for a walk in the rock garden while I finish skinning this fish, and pin my hair up with its bones?" She bows humbly; he takes her hand. Then they are gone.

While they are away from the house, one of the ancestors comes to inquire, "Who is that young woman staying with you?"

"Didn't you know, ancestor," I exclaim, "that my younger sister has just arrived, and will be with us for an extended visit? It is my great delight."

"She does not resemble you, does she?"

"Perhaps it does not leap to the eye, but there is certainly a strong common ground: the basis of our kinship."

"Curious, that I do not remember your mother's second child being born."

"It becomes harder and harder to remember the past, does it not, ancestor?" At last the elder takes her leave.

Later, when they have returned from the garden, we eat our rice on either side of him. He is full of praise for the meal.

"I think I have dropped something under the table," I say; "sister, would you see if you can retrieve it? You cannot find it? Husband, you must help her with your keen sight. I will clear away the dishes."

In the evening, we retire, she to the guest room, he and I to our separate shared room, where the mats are laid next to one another. I sense his restlessness.

"My younger sister," I say to him, "is still not accustomed to the strange new surroundings, the shadow the moon casts in her single room. Used as she is to the large household across the river from which she came, the solitude of darkness cannot be comfortable to her. Do assist her dreams while I unpin my hair. It will not take long until she gathers courage, and is calm enough to sleep."

He goes to do my bidding, and when I myself cannot sleep, I rise and peer through the paper screen, imagining what is behind the silhouette: the broad silk stripe and small pink buds, the velvety petals stroked by hands which move as if arranging flowers. Back in my own room, my shameless ear takes in the tiny moans, which build to the cry I know so well: Having heard the faint echo which follows it, I can at last also sleep, and rest my hand.

X
"Should he consistently seek to conform to the women, it would be a mistake for him."

Every morning since the first on which they had woken together as husband and wife, She Chi and Wei Jen had played a lovers' game. It consisted of a single question. As soon as Wei Jen knew his wife to be awake, he would ask her what in the world she most desired. Her response was often that she already possessed that which she most desired, and flattered and gratified by this response as he was, Wei Jen would persevere, in search of some small thing he could provide her with, some special wish she would be too unselfish to request without his prodding.

"What can I give you today to make you happy?" he asked on this particular morning, and she, with characteristic humility, named nothing. He begged her to think of something, the least thing, that he might do for her, and finally she succumbed.

"Since you insist, Jen," she said reluctantly, "there is in fact something. The pace of our life has been so hectic these last few days; do you not find it so? Today I feel the need for quiet, just one day, undisturbed."

"You shall have it, then, Chi," he said, "your quiet day, and it gives me great pleasure to have this opportunity. We shall not go out, and no guests shall be invited."

"That pleases me, my love, because I am a little weak today," she said. "The pains are with me."

"Why didn't you tell me sooner?" He couldn't bear the thought of her pain, even the mildest pain.

"I will lay a hot compress across your belly," he said, and she let him. He lingered at her side, silent, content, observing her breath. He was beside her a long while.

"Jen," she whispered, "isn't it time for you to visit the emperor, or work in the field, while instead you linger here with me?"

"For you, Chi, all the time in the world," he said, stroking her hands and hair, and more time passed.

"I think it must be day, Jen, I sense the light. How bright it seems already, as if the day would any moment burst. I do not think I could bear the movement."

"Perhaps because you have not eaten, Chi; let me fix you something. Here is a small sesame cake to nibble on while I prepare the rice. Please eat or you will waste away."

"I am a bit hungry now. But if I eat, the pain may be too great, and soon I must be about the day's tasks."

"Lie until you are stronger, Chi. I will wash for you. I will sow the fields, and prepare this evening's meal."

"But surely you are due at the emperor's, for wasn't that the cock crowing just now; it seemed so loud."

"No, love, not yet. You have not rested enough. But do you think you might soon be able to bear the light?"

"Any moment, love. Any day I can."

"Perhaps if you were to eat a little more, but oh, I have burned the rice."

"No, Jen, do not discard it. I know it will be the best I've ever tasted—though I could swear the moon has several times already replaced the sun, and always so much light, that seems to move the dark aside."

"I will put out the candle."

19

"But I am concerned for you, Jen. You will not increase your worldly stature, inactive at my side."

"It is enough to hold you."

"But you will never reincarnate any higher this way, and I am certain now it is the sun, so close at hand."

"I will throw this pebble at it, and if it be instead the moon, then it will suffer only one more indentation."

"But a pebble will not penetrate even one ray of the formidable sun."

"I will extinguish it somehow."

"O love, I swear the cock crows. More than once now."

"I will poison all the animals, and then nothing will disturb you. Can you sleep now?"

"Jen, my beloved, what if they should be tiptoeing into the house this very moment to arrest you for these crimes to the universe on my behalf? I am anxious for you."

"Fear not, Chi, only rest. Shut your eyes. For Wei Jen, close your eyes."

"I know there is movement in the house."

"No love, you only dream. You must dream of sweeter things, fields and flowers, birds and bridges. Try to go to that place, and I will cover you so you are warm enough."

"You do not hear footsteps?"

"That is only the brook gurgling under the bridge, believe me.

"At last she sleeps. And you, so many of you, when one would suffice. I have been expecting you so many hours, or is it days. Please make your steps soft. I will go along without coercion, only do not wake her. Let us all quietly go."

THE STAR CAFÉ

CAROL HEARD A NOISE AS SHE UN-
dressed for bed; it frightened her—she'd actually been half un-
dressing for bed and half searching for the book she had intended
to read in bed, but after she heard the noise she was only a third
involved with each of these tasks and a third involved in trying
to figure out where the noise had come from—though of course
these things could not be measured like sugar or flour; in fact, it
would be more than a third of trying to determine the source of
the sound anyway, because there was fear attached to that fraction, and fear has a way of dispossessing its neighbors. Carol
checked the living room, bathroom and kitchen, and found nothing out of order.

The sound seemed to have come from below her apartment;
the more she thought about it the more right that seemed, and
since she couldn't stop worrying about it, she went back into the
bedroom and slipped into the skirt she'd just taken off, rebuttoned
the blouse she'd never gotten around to removing, was thankful
she hadn't yet taken off underwear, considered putting back on
her shoes but rejected that idea, and walked into the living room
again, toward the door.

As she was undoing the latch, she saw on the small table
between door and sofa the book she'd been looking for; it must
have been there all along. She picked it up so as not to misplace
it again, and opened the door. On the landing she heard the
noise a second time. Though she'd been expecting it, it startled
her anew, so much so that she dropped the book, then watched
it tumble to the second-to-last step.

23

The hallway was dark and the darkness had intensified the sound. It was dark because the light switch was located on the wall opposite the bannister at the bottom of the stairs, and she hadn't gotten there yet because she'd been interrupted by the sound; she was still standing there at fearful attention, like a deer with a flashlight shining in its eyes, as if stillness were some kind of defense instead of vulnerability.

Carol wondered why there wasn't a switch at the top landing as well as at the bottom. Perhaps the architect was biased toward those ascending? Or would it be the electrician? She knew so little about these practical matters; she knew so little about this building she lived in. If she had to guess when it had been built, she might have erred in the region of decades rather than single years. What she did know was that there was far too little light for a building with so many windows, all located on its tree-blocked western exposure.

The noise had stopped but Carol couldn't get it out of her head. It seemed to become clearer rather than less clear in proportion to time elapsed since its occurrence. But how could someone really know if the hold she had on what had been heard or seen or felt was really becoming clearer, that is, truer, or more distorted? Was intensity a proper gauge? Wasn't it often the case that those who felt most enlightened were in fact most deluded?

Then she heard it again, not memory or imagination. It had to be coming from somewhere downstairs, and she had to go downstairs, if only to retrieve her book, so she slowly descended, thinking that it was really the simplest sound, so why so difficult to characterize? It only seemed eerie because she didn't know the source, she kept telling herself.

When she reached the bottom of the staircase, Carol stood a moment, then sat down on the penultimate step, next to her book, listening to the sound that still hadn't stopped—its duration was the longest of the three occurrences—trying to get up the courage to go open the door that led to the little restaurant she'd lived above for all these months but never entered. The mixture of curiosity and fright had led her this far, she could hardly give up now; the noise might stop again any second and then it would be harder to trace. She walked down the hall and stood against the door with her hand curled on the knob, as if she were holding a piece of fruit still attached to a branch.

She placed the sound the instant she opened the door. The first time she heard it she should have known what it was. Who would have thought an innocent little blender—well, not so little, really, larger, in fact, than any she'd ever seen; she guessed it could hold several gallons—but who would have thought it could make such a queer noise, an innocent if somewhat oversized blender, making what looked like banana daiquiris? She giggled, and suddenly realized she wasn't alone, that she was being scrutinized by a man—a waiter?—more likely the owner, an extremely handsome man in all the conventional ways: dark and tall, both noble and rugged. He switched off the mighty appliance, poured a fraction of its contents into a long-stemmed glass, held that out to her and smiled.

"Hello, Carol," he said.

She was so relieved by the release of all that tension that she suddenly wanted, urgently, to talk to him, though it could have been to anyone, any sympathetic ear into which she could expel what had been building up inside her. She found herself babbling about how pleased she was to have the mystery solved; she was glad it was only that. He listened attentively, but rarely responded. Perhaps she didn't give him much chance.

He was looking at her intently from behind the counter, and when she felt too uncomfortable to confront his gaze directly she stared at the travel posters that adorned the wall behind him. She must have imagined that his eyes were unusually bright; it was her weariness, it was the candlelight, but for some reason she felt compelled. She was telling him all these things about herself, all the silly thoughts, the things about the architect and the light fixture, how they'd been so long next door to each other and never known each other better, and really she'd never done anything like this before but she was letting him hold her; first he had held her hand and then suddenly she was in his arms, he was murmuring softly, "yes, yes," consoling her, reassuring her, stroking her hair, and then other parts of her, and before she knew it she found herself in bed with him, in the back room, which was not so sordid as it might sound. There was a bed and all the accouterments of civilized sexuality, of comfort; it wasn't after all a closet, but she wondered what he would do if a customer came in, and then she began to wonder why there weren't customers out there. There hadn't been any when she came in, nor all the time they'd been, or she'd been, talking; she'd run on so about up and down and stairs and light; she'd been overwhelmed, full of herself in a way quite foreign to her, though there was also the sense that she was acting out a role that came very naturally, almost as if she'd rehearsed it, and she wondered if all this was the thing people always meant by the term "attraction," "I'm so attracted to you," as if people were magnets, which would be at least somewhat specific, or if she was just needy because of the fright, and lonely, lonely for a long time now, which would be at least not entirely, merely physical.

In either case she wasn't proud of herself; it was strange to be in bed with a man she barely knew, though in those minutes of talking it seemed there was some intense acquaintanceship occurring. It was strange to be in bed with someone at all, she'd been alone so long, almost out of habit; the "with" of "in bed with" was the important part of the construction, to be in the presence of another human being, because the sex came naturally enough; the angels never really withheld that.

Awkwardness granted, the motions materialized, to such a degree, in fact, that she felt she was experiencing far more than just going through them. She couldn't remember such satisfying sex; was it just the novelty? But everything clicked. She felt that they'd held each other's bodies for years and every gesture had the right timbre and timing, but with none of the staleness that might characterize the context. It was perfect but also felt, not slick. She certainly felt, and it seemed the kind of feeling that could not exist except reciprocally. It was as if they were lovers reunited after a long separation, fitting easily into place again. What was passion if not this? She slept a blissful, sated sleep.

When she woke up, she was alone. Everywhere around her were mirrors. The way school buses have mirrors to cover every possible vantage, this room, from her position on the bed, allowed her to see her body from every angle. She was fascinated by this, and distracted for quite a while, but then began to be afraid. She couldn't find her way past the immediate space around her. It reminded her of fancy New York stores in which it is difficult to find one's way because the different departments are separated by walls of mirrors.

Suddenly he was there in the mirrors. She was extremely moved that he'd come to be with her there, to rescue her; for some reason she was certain that he wasn't trapped by the situation, but had purposefully navigated to it, to get to her. Her first impulse was to take his hand and run with him out of this world of reflection, but he didn't lead her out; instead, to her shock, he climbed on top of her—what could be less appropriate?—at least out of sequence; that came after the rescue, in the gratitude and relief stage, while here she was, still a captive of this reflective dragon. But as the weight of his body pressed against her, she decided she'd been wrong; it was completely appropriate. She was so tied to her sense of propriety. There was no need to leave the place right now; no exits would seal while he entered—which happened so quickly she was startled, but startled at how *un*startled her body was, unkindled but still receptive—he taught her so much by his body.

He was thrusting in her so energetically it should have hurt, but it didn't, or if it did, the hurt was subsumed in the intensity of pleasure and excitement she felt. She had an orgasm as intense as any she had ever experienced, and felt after as if she could never have another, intense or otherwise, but just as she was thinking that he turned her over onto her belly and came into her from behind, and she heard herself make sounds she had never heard from her own mouth, in response to this pleasure on the crest of saturation.

She made them all the way to her second orgasm, not a very long way, in fact, and then there were others; she'd always thought that a myth. Only as she was coming did she remember the erotic potential of this room or space she was in—she'd been so overwhelmed with sensations and feeling that it hadn't occurred to her to heighten the effect with the visual; she was angry at herself to have missed out on that; when would she ever have such an opportunity again.

She loved the idea of watching their bodies in conjunction with each other, of him pressing into her. She turned to look back over her shoulder so that she could see him disappearing into her, and then turned her head in order to be able to see without straining, in all the mirrors. Her orgasm, at its most intense point, was retracted. The cry that rose from her throat continued, though perhaps the pitch changed just slightly, or the quality of the sound; maybe only she could hear the difference, that it wasn't from pleasure or surfeit anymore but from shock and bewilderment, because in all the mirrors she was there writhing—she could see her breasts and belly and legs, all from underneath, as if there were no bed obstructing; she could also see herself from his vantage; she could see what someone opening a door, if there were a door, would see, from far away, with the head prominent and the hair draped over the bed; she could see her shoulders and back, but he was not depicted in any of these images. She lay on the bed without partner. She felt humiliated and horrified, and guilty too, though she couldn't have said why.

She had no idea how to attack this problem with relation to the other person who might or might not be present. It was an extreme case of some kind of sexual etiquette. The problem was, she didn't know this man, the café owner, at all; she knew him no better than she'd know a blind date, and yet they were sharing, weren't they, this intimate circumstance. Everything had felt so natural before; she'd let the sensation absorb any uncomfortableness, but now she was too disturbed by his absence from the mirror to retrieve her passion, and she felt too silly or shy to inquire about it directly.

Would he think she was crazy, or was he somehow manipulating his own image for some sinister reasons she had no idea of? Oh, why did she ever with this perfect stranger, and hadn't he seemed it in both senses of the term, but now she would pay. What would her mother say, who'd always been so cautiously liberal . . . "Carol, if you don't know a man's last name, you don't know him well enough to . . ." Thus what had seemed the most natural thing in the world suddenly de-naturalized and was transformed into the most awkward. How could she carry on this charade, when she possessed private knowledge that her partner was missing? It was just ludicrous to continue and at the same time witness the bleak absurdity of her body making love to the atmosphere. The postures could be made to look ridiculous enough even with both parties attending, but then at least they were salvaged by familiarity. Maybe the act itself was unnatural, maybe this was some elaborate lesson for her. She could be alone the rest of her life; she knew how.

She couldn't ask him what he saw in the mirror; she wished she could be so direct, but they hadn't spoken since that initial conversation, which might as well have taken place in some other world. She could feel the motions going on in some removed physical dimension, but to a very different effect. She was numb now, throughout her body; she wondered if he'd notice; he must notice. Was he intending all this, and should she then try her best to play along to try to counter-trick—how appalling to have to think in terms of strategy in such circumstances—pretending she really did see him in the mirror? Or was this some entirely different conspiracy of the elements in which he was as innocent as she? But was she? How could she be in such a terrible predicament if she hadn't done something terribly wrong; yes, it was repression and all the rest, but really, this kind of thing didn't happen to the average person. Confront, evade, despair? She didn't know which to do.

She'd never in her life faked an orgasm, as women were supposed to be notorious for, and she hadn't had so many either; in fact these recent ones constituted more than a small percentage of the total, but to do precisely that suddenly seemed the best plan, to get it all over with, so that this beginning-to-be-very-oppressive weight would be removed, and she wouldn't have to continue doing this thing, performing these movements, which are by definition directed toward another, to no one. She even managed to make some noise; she was surprised at how convincing it sounded, having expected the artificiality to be glaring. The trouble was, he took no notice; she might have spared herself the trouble—he wasn't through. Then she realized that she hadn't noticed if he had yet had one to her many, how selfish of her; she'd been caught up in the intensity of her own pleasure. But he seemed insatiable. It felt so odd, and now it was the etiquette thing amplified thousands of times, because she wanted say, "Excuse me, do you think you'll be through soon?" as if to someone at a pay phone, except she had made all her calls and just wanted to hear the receiver click.

As she looked at her body now, it was limp and tense at once, receiving the invisible—less absurd than what she'd seen in the heat of her solitary passion, but still pathetic. Maybe there was a device analogous to the one-way mirror: a half-mirror, in which only one party at a time was visible. Such a thing could exist. So now the big question was, did he see only himself, the same way she saw only herself? How simple it all was; she was immensely relieved for the second time in—how many hours had this been going on?—she had no idea, but was overjoyed to realize that the sum of their perceptions would yield a complete love-making couple; she thought she might cry with the relief of it. Suddenly it was as it had been back in the café; she had invented all the problems; she was ashamed at having suspected him. She wanted to tell him everything and have him say, "Silly thing," and stroke her, make it all better.

But he didn't say that and she was still trapped underneath him: this man she was not with despite his presence. It was happening to someone else; he was inside someone else, who only happened to be Carol. Who cared about sex? She'd give up sex forever; just get her out of here. She yearned for nothing so much as the removal of this corporeal hook whose eye she was. Oh, give her the pain; she'd rather that, to feel her body affirming the wrongness of what was being done to/in it, the participation that pain was, rather than this numbness, distance, this irrevocable breach with the action she was party to.

She was exhausted now. Maybe she could cry so much that her body would force itself to sleep and when she woke up it would be normal, because that was the way things had worked till now; why shouldn't it solve itself so simply? But how could it when the situation had changed so drastically? She had not chosen this. Everything was different; he wasn't the same he; she herself—oh, was she also different, not just in the sense of having learned something, but substantially altered? Could she not go home again even to the home of her being? Was it going to prove that large a crime she'd committed, to herself, or invited if not committed: some psychic leaving of the keys in the car, or the house unlocked? Take from me; violate me? But no, how could she have known that the locks would not only be changed by the time she got home, but in her impotent presence the lock, the whole house changed, the door, the windows, the stairs (how long ago it seemed she'd stood at the top of her stairway) all turned inside out and impossible to put back in order.

That's when he stopped. Vision was the only sense that informed her, because feeling had long since been used up. The point was that nothing was different after he stopped, the same way on a long trip you feel like you're driving even after you get out of the car. She wanted to know what it was that made that particular point the one he'd selected as enough. Maybe he'd climaxed. But she suspected he had a completely different kind of sexuality, not based on that system. Even if it was the same system it was different, because no man ever took that long to get to the point conventionally regarded as completion; no ordinary man. Or had she drawn it out in her mind because she was so uncomfortable? No, there couldn't be that much disparity.

He was leaving. He had dismounted and left the bed. It seemed that he didn't need any time to recover from his own experience. He was walking away and she was free, no longer oppressed by that weight, that invasion; she'd been granted just what she pleaded for. But what would she do, if he left her all alone in the room again, with no one and no way out and no way of knowing where? She was more afraid than ever.

"Oh please don't go," she said. "Don't leave me alone. I'm afraid to be alone here."

Her request wasn't on the order of begging the lover to linger a little longer, wanting to draw out his sweet company, not Juliet bemoaning the lark song; it was simply preferring any risk to the risk of solitude, the way someone you're suspicious of suddenly seems harmless when you see the real villain. But she was only half involved with this anxiety about his departure, probably more than half, that is, not entirely consumed by the fear, because she was partly caught up in watching him begin to dress, seeing his body for the first time from a distance, with perspective. And she was also ashamed at feeling renewed attraction for this man whom she'd minutes ago felt utterly victimized by. But she couldn't get over his beauty; at this moment she wasn't so much aroused by the sight of him naked as interested in his body aesthetically.

She dwelled upon the refined features: cheekbones, throat, his beautiful hands. Her own hands had felt the softness of his dark hair, from that of his head to the field that pooled below his navel. He was fuzzy and nice down there, she remembered the feeling of that against her. Before she had only seen him hard,

now she found it just as appealing soft; she supposed he wouldn't
appreciate that sentiment, he would surely not deviate from the
norm in that respect. She also wondered if it was abnormal of
her to feel as she did, not to prefer it hard.

They had been united by that organ; now it was just a part
of him again; perhaps it had its own little memory, its own will,
and was choosing now to disassociate itself from the warm surround she had provided. And how she had soared in the first
stages of that providing. She'd never had such a strong sense of
being with a man: that she was the feminine to his masculine.
He elicited from her a quality of her own femaleness that she'd
never before experienced on that physical plane—a response she
realized might be hopelessly bound up in the conditioning of
role, but was nonetheless immensely powerful. It was getting clear
again, with the distance, with his going, the power of the sensation
that had made her respond in a way she never had: totally. She'd
come outside herself to meet him through the medium of body,
through the act of letting him inside her, and yet never felt so
fully in her body, in her self, as when she had.

He was working now toward his clothes: a neat pile con-
trasting with her own things, scattered around it. She didn't remember him taking off what he was now putting on; she thought
they were the same clothes he'd been wearing when they first
met and talked. It was a button-down shirt, that much she remembered, but the color looked a little different than it had in
the candlelight: pale pink oxford cloth; it might look effeminate
on most men but on him it was just right, perfect for his blend
of beauty and masculinity, his refined masculinity.

As she was observing him in the act of dressing, deep in her
own reflections, she felt quite spontaneously in her genitals the
muscular contractions of orgasm. She'd been concentrating on
the pinkness of the shirt, and watching him put his firm,
muscular—first right, then left—legs into his gray flannel trousers
in a business-like manner, when out of nowhere her body had

produced this gratuitous release to no accumulated tension, in an instant of incredible intensity that left her completely drained, as if she'd been building up to it for some time. She'd often wished she could speed up that process but this was a most undesirable other extreme, this joyless, arbitrary orgasm; it was in no way satisfying. If anything, scary. This very strange ventriloquism made her furious. For the first time toward him she felt her emotions focus as unmitigated, almost violent anger. She felt used, much more so even than when he had been doing to her what technically could be considered rape. But to do this intimate thing from across the room! How cowardly of him; that's what it was, truly unmanly, that he wouldn't even face her with his body to manipulate her, though in a way it was honest, to be so blatant.

A marvelous thing indeed it would be if she could think her way to orgasm, or come just by watching him, but this was quite different, as removed a process as artificial insemination, this artificial climax for which she had been just the vehicle. She wanted to hit him but she was practically incapacitated as a result of her climax. She wanted to hit him because she felt stunned as if she had been struck; she had fallen back from an upright position, and as she'd fallen back, her peripheral vision had received the mirror's version of that moment. It contained two genders; a man's reflection had been for that instant there: a single thrust by all the reflected men in all the mirrors: multiple petals around her lonely, central, actual pistil, from which no bee sucked nectar. Why was she surprised, that they would contradict no matter what, turn appearances around as a matter of course? She should have the pattern down by now.

A few minutes later she had her strength back, but since immediacy would have been the point, there was no use in striking him now. It would probably only end up hurting her anyway. Alternatively she decided to maintain utter dignity, which was difficult because she needed to go to the bathroom and there wasn't a chance she'd be able to divine the whereabouts of the ladies' room. She got off the bed in as stately a manner as she could accomplish and walked slowly but deliberately to where he stood. She tried not to feel vulnerable despite the fact that she was naked and he now completely clothed.

"There's a matter of some urgency," she said.

He looked up at her. "If you want to leave," he said, "all you have to do is figure it out. No one will stop you. I certainly won't."

After she had held her breath a minute, determined not to start crying, she tried again: "That's not the matter I had in mind—something much more mundane. You see, I have to, I need to [he was no help] find a bathroom."

"There aren't any." He wasn't very gracious.

"Oh," she said, at a loss. Then she found courage.

"Look, you have to help me."

She was afraid he wouldn't answer, and was thankful when he finally said, as if he'd been thinking about it all the while rather than ignoring her as she'd thought, "In fact, there is something," and hastened to add, "but it's only meant to be decoration. It was part of the architect's design."

Since her urgency was not decreasing she couldn't afford to be choosy. Responding to her expectant look, he led her to an alcove she could have sworn had not existed, but then it was hard to tell because of all the reflection. In any case she hadn't noticed this place before. Somehow the mirrors masked the contours. It was hard to tell how far the room extended, hard to distinguish what was reflection from what was actual space.

"This is all I have," he said (what a funny salesman he'd make, she thought), gesturing toward two gleaming urinals, affixed to the wall at waist height, totally out of place though in another way consistent with the atmosphere.

"Are you going to watch?" she asked in an injured tone, and he accommodatingly turned to walk away, but then she called him back and asked him to give her a hand, being pragmatic rather than proud.

"Help me," she said, but it was a question rather than a statement because she didn't know exactly what she wanted him to do for her, or whether he would even know how to help her. She had in mind a position that would somehow enable her to put feminine function into masculine form. She stood on tiptoe and stepped backward, facing him—she did not want to have her back to him—until she straddled the fixture. It was difficult to do this, but not impossible because she, although not tall, had fairly long legs, and the thing itself was not all that high. The insides of her thighs made contact with the porcelain rim; it was cold, but she couldn't raise herself high enough to avoid it.

She was still looking at him for some kind of assistance, and he, regarding her now as if she were truly demented, approached her, reaching his hand out hesitantly, as if he felt obliged to offer it but didn't know quite where to touch her, how to hold or support her. Finally he squatted in front of her and the urinal, and grasped her legs just above the knee, as one might hold a ladder someone else is standing on, to make it secure. This was no help. It was so strange to have him touching her in this functional way; she realized she didn't want him to touch her at all. Certainly she didn't want him to witness her in the actual act of urinating, especially in this awkward posture, and she couldn't wait much longer. Perhaps realizing that he was making no contribution, he rose, but kept standing there, out of malice or ignorance she wasn't sure: his face was blank.

"Thanks for the help," she said, hoping he would take that as dismissal.

He looked mesmerized by her sustained acrobatic—an expression foreign to his face as she knew it: being in the power of something rather than being in power over something, someone. Then he snapped out of it, looked normal again, and said, "The needs of his guest are a host's first priority." Was he sneering, or was it her own distortion of his smile? Then he turned quickly away. They seemed far from anything sexual now, poles apart from each other's sexuality. It was as if her nakedness were the most ordinary thing in the world to him now. At least he was gone and she could urinate in peace, if not exactly comfort, since relief was thwarted by the awkwardness of posture. There was so little space between her and the fixture that she got splashed by little droplets. Well, it's sterile anyway, she thought. Of course there was nothing to wipe herself with; there were no accessories to this monstrosity. It vaguely resembled a baptismal font.

She eased herself off, gripping the sides for support; this time she didn't have to worry about looking dignified. Once on land again, dry, flat land, she spread her legs, planting her feet far apart, and waved her hand rapidly between her thighs to speed up the air-drying process, as she leaned against the cold porcelain, too cold to keep contact with for any longer than necessary. She was tired of being in discomfort. Hadn't she suffered enough? She stopped leaning and tried fanning with no support but found her legs still too unstable, so she compromised by kneeling, though that didn't leave much space in which to wave her hand. All her muscles ached now; she wanted to find the bed again and lie down, but she couldn't summon the energy. Fatigue overcame any squeamishness she had about lying on the floor near the urinals: he had said they were only used as decoration. She lay on her back, at first with her legs up, positioned like an open scissor, as in one of the exercises she did, to facilitate fanning, which her left hand had taken over. The absurdity of the whole endeavor suddenly struck her; she dropped her legs to the floor, exhaled, and closed her eyes, vowing she would allow herself the luxury for only a minute. It might have been several minutes, before she was seized by panic. Where had he gone when she'd sent him away? She forgot about her fatigue and ran into the main part of the room, trying not to bump into glass. He was nowhere. As she was about to call him she realized she had no name for him. Oh, what a fool she was, alone just as she'd feared, and all her own fault. How useless everything was.

But she wouldn't let herself cry—no more despair. It was time to be practical, at least to go through the motions of being practical, for her own sake, to try to create some sense, even a contrived one, of order, in this most peculiar, relentless universe.

So she began to dress, even though there was no rational reason to do so, except to feel dignified, and what else was there to do? She looked fondly at her scattered clothes. She regarded them as a soldier might some article that had been with him through numerous battles. And who knew what battles were yet to come, she thought, almost saying it out loud to her faithful skirt and blouse, the ones she'd been in the process of removing when she left her bedroom to investigate, the thing that got her into this nightmare: her fear of the sound, followed by her—feeling—for the café owner.

On some level she knew she was an intuitive person, but she hadn't learned to trust herself, too cautious, as if there were a very strong force at work inside her all the time that wasn't allowed to come to expression, like all that sun missing her house, all this foliage in her head, that was so pretty and interesting and alive, but how much it got in the way. She suspected that her mind had evolved in some distorted fashion, different from the rest of the world. And now here she was, trapped in this stagnancy of glass, that had become by all its clarity a blur, itself a distortion. She couldn't forgive herself, though she supposed she'd suffered enough to be redeemed of any number of sins or crimes. She cursed her intuition, because she'd never have stayed with him if she'd weighed, considered, evaluated. On the other hand, she'd never do anything if she always weighed, considered, evaluated; that was precisely what so often kept her from doing any number of things, things she felt a genuine desire to do, but couldn't get over this habit or obsession of getting stuck, nothing resolving itself. She felt the irony of the whole thing as deeply, as physically, as a metallic taste in her mouth: that the only time she'd ever felt not removed from her body, when will and act had meshed, was with him; it had felt so right, but clearly had been wrong, as wrong as anything could be. She slid the tab of the zipper all the way up and fastened the button at the waistband of her skirt, then leaned against one of the mirrors as she dreamily repeated the motion of button through opening, gentle grasps and pulls, all the way up her blouse. If only there were as simple a motion to secure her exit. He had said she had only to figure it out. And there had to be a door; somewhere there had to be. She thrust her weight hard against the mirror as she leaned, then moved forward to tuck in her blouse. Had the mirror seemed to give a little as she had pressed? She must be imagining it. Perhaps if she pushed against every mirror, one of them might yield.

In the café, he poured her a drink, yellow, creamy stuff from the blender into a large, stemmed glass. He held it high as he poured, the way waiters had poured milk for her in restaurants when she'd been young; she'd been impressed at how high they could go and still not spill. She fumbled in her pocket for change, feeling stupid, not knowing where she stood. He put his hands over hers and said, "On the house."

"Oh," she said softly. "Thank you."

She had no idea what role she was playing. Was she customer, or worse, had he been hers? It was so different, he was nice again. His demeanor toward her suggested that they were only now about to be lovers, romantic, but she knew they'd already been, and what had gone on had had little to do with romance. She wasn't making much progress with the daiquiri, taking occasional nervous gulps, clutching the glass.

"It's different now," she said with desperate bravery.

"Same ingredients as always," he replied. "Are you sure you've had one before?" The way he smiled made her nervous. This was more confusing than ever.

Too uncomfortable to look at him, she kept surveying the room and its contents: the candles, the fancy Breuer chairs, all the bottles and glasses lined along shelves on the mirrored wall of the bar, a large quilt that somehow fit in with the rest of the decor; the central part of its design was a large star—it took her a minute to realize it was there because of the name of the place: the Star Café. The quilt took up almost all of one wall; the other walls were decorated with posters, mostly from museum exhibits.

There were the travel posters as well, one a sophisticated montage of tourists and countryside in Greece, each scene in a separate little box. On the bottom was Greek lettering. She had always wanted to go there; it seemed like such a magical place, not just in some superficial sense of island and sun (one of the little boxes showed tourists lying on a beach) though that was appealing, and not just in the sense of the magic of the past either, being surrounded by ancient history; her sense was of a magic that was also chthonic. That was the world of myth, of gods and goddesses, of honor and heroism, justice, revenge. That was a much larger world than her own, she felt, that company of furies and sirens in which choice was fate, and fate was really everything, but no matter what brutality caused by what whim of some god's arbitrary favoritism, reliable rosy-fingered dawn was always waiting in the wings to make it all into poetry. She was enamored of that civilization which was a celebration of the splendor of form. She thought of the perfection of body that lived in those white marble statues, the strength and grace which rhymed for her with his body, the body that had mingled with her own, but was now so distant. She needed to know that it had.

"Were you ever there?" she asked him, not even asking for understanding so much as simple information.

"Once, years ago," he said, "but it's too dirty and the food's too greasy. I like a more antiseptic atmosphere; Scandinavia's more to my taste."

Willfully or inadvertently he had taken her to be referring to the travel poster. She resented this glib distortion of her meaning. He had no right to be so evasive. Or had he just misunderstood? He had no right not to understand. Anger supplanted her nervousness so that now she had no trouble looking directly at him. But he wasn't looking at her; he was eyeing the blender, and before she could challenge him he was onto that as the new topic, as if his little remark had been an adequate response to her searching question, and no more need be said about it. What nearly disarmed her was the tenderness with which he said, when he looked back at her, "How sweet that you were afraid of my blender, silly thing."

That was just what she would have wanted to hear before, but not now that she'd been through what she'd been through, an experience of suffering so vivid that it created a landscape in her mind as powerful as the mythical one in which she had just been lost. In fact they became one for her at this moment, she could envision her own story painted across some urn, the woman whose lover wasn't there, in little scenes that reminded her of the travel poster, except that they weren't photographed and weren't in boxes, little red figures depicted on the urn: Carol in her apartment, then going downstairs, then in the bar, Carol in bed, then in the mirrored room, Carol looking in the mirrors, him there, him not there, but Carol crouching in the urinal was really too squalid for the likes of any Grecian urn, and now, with her imagination engrossed in this world that did not take passion lightly, that addressed mortality and immortality as real concerns rather than abstractions, and raised to the highest pitch the difference and link between the two—now, it was grossly inadequate, even pathetic.

"I'm not your silly thing," she blurted out, and he seemed taken aback by her anger.

"What's got into you?" he asked.

"Stop pretending you don't know," she said. "You know what I'm talking about. Tell me if you were there or not."

"I've already told you . . ." he began, but she cut him off. She was very worked up now.

"When I ask if you were there, I mean were you with me, in the room? I mean I know you were with me, but what I'm asking is . . . why are you trying to make me think I was imagining you?" This speech was delivered *crescendo ed accelerando*. "You owe it to me to tell me!" She was very excited and annoyed to realize she had to urinate again. She must have managed to get down more of that daiquiri than she thought.

"Yes," he said quietly.

"What do you mean yes? You can't say yes or no if I ask you, was it a, b, or c. I need a specific answer. Was it real or my imagination?"

"Yes!" This time it wasn't quiet.

He didn't look like someone playing games; he looked tortured himself, but she was sure he must be trying to get away with something.

"You're being cryptic again," she said. "You're trying to confuse me. And I need the ladies' room; does that ring a bell? I may as well tell you that it's illegal not to have one in a public eating place, so don't try to tell me there isn't any."

"You think you're so smart," he raised his voice to match hers. "I have something to tell you too. There is, technically speaking, no ladies' room. There is, however, one rest-room, androgynous, past the bar and to your right."

She began the journey immediately. When she'd taken only a few steps he called to her, by name, for the first time since that very first time.

"Carol!"

She turned around.

"We're through."

That was fine with her; she turned away again directly and continued on the prescribed route. Once through a corridor she found the door immediately to her right, marked simply "rest." She opened it, entered, and shut it behind her, pushing in the little circle in the middle of the knob to lock it, then tried to jiggle the knob to make sure. She realized how silly that was; who was she locking out? The man who had seen and known her body to the full extent of possibility between human beings? But locking it made her feel better. The interior was clean enough; she would have tried to hold out if it hadn't been. This bathroom was extremely clean, in fact, so she didn't feel the need to get in and out as quickly as possible. It was mirrored, of course, mirrored tiles on the walls and floor. Also the ceiling. The toilet and sink were ordinary. A fresh bar of soap lay in the dish on the arm of the sink—so much nicer than powdery stuff out of a dispenser, she thought. How good it would feel to have clean hands. She rubbed the soap between her palms for a long time, working up a rich lather with warm water from the faucet. She decided to wash her face as well; she hadn't had the opportunity in so long. She held her hair with one hand but couldn't completely avoid getting it wet. She didn't mind; she would happily have dunked her whole head into the basin for the feel of this welcome refreshment.

In fact, why stop there, she thought, and pulled her blouse off over her head. She felt sweaty and horrible; scrubbing some soap under her arms would make her feel a little better, since she couldn't shower. She unhooked the closure in front of her bra and slipped the straps down her arms one at a time with her wet hand. In the mirror she stared at her small breasts, and was pleased with them. Her nipples were hard. She rubbed the soap vigorously under her arms, then rinsed, trying to stand over the sink in such a way that the least water would spill on the floor.

She had forgotten to check for a towel before she started; there was none, so she dabbed herself dry with pieces of toilet paper. She'd almost forgotten about her urgency; she'd make some superficial attempt at washing of genitalia after. She pulled down her panties, stepped out of them and hung them on a hook she'd just noticed protruding from the door. She rescued her blouse from where it had fallen and hung that too. She gathered up her skirt with her right hand, intending to sit on the toilet, but was distracted by suddenly seeing herself in the mirrored wall, as if seeing another person. She looked at this person who held her skirt in her arms so that it draped her hips but revealed her belly, fur and thighs. Her breasts were still uncovered also, and just as she had found them adequate, satisfying, she now found this lower region of her body, in fact the whole body, cut off as it was at the waist—she found the entire image attractive.

She stood transfixed by this lovely landscape under canopy of skirt. Her flesh seemed firmer than she remembered, more muscle

43

tone; maybe the exercises she'd been doing in the morning and before bedtime had finally paid off. It had been hard to motivate herself to do them, with no prospect of anyone to appreciate the results, since she'd had no way of knowing about the café owner. She couldn't have predicted that, though as it was happening, there had been, in the midst of all that anguish and terror and pleasure, a tiny seed of déjà vu; that was a common phenomenon, of course.

Well, it didn't make much difference in the end, did it? She knew that she often allowed herself to become the victim of her own speculations, reflections. Now it all seemed unimportant compared to the immediacy of the woman in the mirror, the urgency of that woman's sexuality or physicality. Strange to feel genuinely aroused by this image of herself. She amused herself with the idea that it was perfectly logical for her to associate her unaccompanied reflection with arousal, since that had been the consistent image during her definitive sexual experience.

Now the woman in the mirror was touching herself, sliding her palm up her thigh, transferring the skirt to the guardianship of the left hand. Then she left skin to approach her breasts. She caressed them fervently, then left skin again to return below the skirt, lingering for a long time when the hand met flesh again, languidly rubbing the soft pubic hair, just a shade darker than the honey-colored hair of her head, which fell away from her shoulders, skimming the floor as she bent low for the mirror.

The mirror-woman did a seductive dance, holding the skirt tight across her hips, swaying; she watched the curve of her calves as she gracefully inscribed the area of the bathroom floor, often lifting her leg so high that her lips were visible.

She was extremely aroused by this time, and not ashamed of it; she wanted to possess this beautiful moving image. She felt a fullness in her groin, decided it was her old need to urinate, which seemed less and less urgent; she couldn't be bothered with addressing that now—it was confusing how similar that feeling was with that of being sexually excited. She was rubbing herself, much more vigorously than was her habit; she let the skirt drop to have both hands. She tried to put one finger of her free hand inside herself but couldn't gain entry, despite the fact that she was very wet by now. It wasn't necessary anyway, and she was happy enough to have access to both hands for rubbing.

She was so tensed and excited that her vision was blurred; she'd lost the mirror's reflection, but it was firmly fixed in her mind; she dwelled on all the postures, the confronting gaze, the beauty and sensuality of that body. She needed some kind of support, weak from so much excitement. When leaning against the sink proved insufficient she quickly closed the lid of the toilet and sat there.

Under the skirt she rubbed so fast that her hand was tiring, so she supported the right with the left, cupped the two and stroked, leaning back against the tank. She recalled there must be semen in her still, if he had come, that is, but he must have come, at least once, and probably generously, he had to have, it just wasn't possible—she felt it coming out of her, not just dribbling but in spurts, as she herself climaxed. She cried out with the new pleasure of it, an intense, confined pleasure, as she felt suddenly claustrophobic; she needed air, even if it was just the air of the corridor. She rose and unlocked the door by turning the knob hard, opened it and stuck her head out, like a seasick traveler leaning out a porthole; she saw down the length of the corridor into the room with the bar, where it had all begun. Directly in the line of her vision was the poster of Greece; it was far away, and the contents of the little boxes were fuzzy, like the last letters of the eye-doctor's chart, but she could see rocks and white sand, and tall, white columns. She was drawn toward them, she wanted to see every box clearly; her nakedness did not inhibit her for some reason. He didn't matter so much anymore; she wouldn't let him keep her from exploring. There was nothing to be embarrassed about. No one was there.

MATERIA PRIMA

Every thursday, it was the custom in my family to have something of a social, nostalgic evening. My aunts and uncles would come for dinner, bringing along their children, one of whom was very close to my age, and when the discussion began to bore or exclude us, we would slip away to have more private congress. But we had more of a taste for adult ambiance than most children, and didn't leave until well after the dishes were cleared and the men's cigars lit, the photo albums brought out, and the anecdotes had begun to recycle.

Our presence was tolerated, encouraged to a degree, but less our participation, for the maxim that stipulated children be visual, nonaudible entities ruled our home, and if it was less the case in my cousin's, when in Rome they did as we did.

Thus any sustained attempt on my or my cousin Laura's part—and more often it was on mine—to reactivate the past by interpolating ourselves into the conversation was almost certain to lead to banishment. Still I couldn't resist. Children are notoriously vain in that they have allegedly no interest in events which predate them, or in pictures which do not contain their images, but I would have been satisfied with even indirect access to the mysterious adult world.

I remember occasions on which a photograph was shown or a story told, and one particular image or name would spark a series of images, sensations or memories. Other times it was a simple factual correspondence; remembering a place or person which or who had been dormant prior to this catalystic action,

49

but if I made the mistake of exclaiming over such knowledge, my mother or father would invariably say, more to the rest of the company than to me, "Clara, you couldn't possibly remember that far back. You were just a baby." Or, worse yet, "Why, you weren't even born yet." End of discussion. Only one's parents can steal past and present irrevocably in one dismissive blow.

we live in a very big brick building near the road a special also very big road that takes everyone into the city and back again to where their house is. our building is right near one of the green signs that tell cars where to get on or off and there is lots of traffic because so many people live in the building like we do different floors of it. we are way way up and the only way to get there is taking the elevator. it scared me at first but papa said it is safe it works by cables. I don't know who cables are but they are less scary than thinking it goes all by itself up and down in the air.

sometimes I take it all alone when I am allowed to get our mail from a metal box in the lobby room vestibule mama says say vestibule and that happens when I am lucky because mama trusts me with the silver baby key that opens our box where the mail lives. if all the mothers feel like trusting all the children at the same time we go outside together in a big group to walk or ride bicycles. we don't go very far.

inside in what is named apartment even though it is where we are together I have a little room which is nice when I feel like being just with me. the kitchen is warm and has a window that sees the park. my room's window only sees the brick sides of the next door building. I like mama and papa's room best my favorite thing is to lie in bed with them all warm and snuggly between but one night I hear them fighting about this.

our rooms are so next to each other that I can hear so I go to get a glass of milk in the kitchen and drop the glass bottle by mistake because I am listening so hard I forget to be careful holding. it lands on my toe and makes it bleed. they come to see *what happened and yell a little. mama washes the cut while papa calls on the phone and then carries me to the car so I can go get stitches in the middle of the night. the stitches hurt more than the glass did especially the big needle to make it not hurt that comes first but I am more scared of mama and papa knowing I was trying to listen. sometimes I think they want to change things so I'm not always there to hear things. it will all change anyway when I go to school which is soon I think.*

I suppose I was overly sensitive to these blows, which I interpreted as insults, and suppose also that my recollection was merely imagined or invented of a desire to be included, but I couldn't help feeling slighted and diminished to have this vivid landscape, actual or otherwise, be, at the very moment of its conjuring, stolen back and declared invalid, as if the madeleine had been snatched from Proust's mouth.

I don't think I would have been half as hurt had their denial been conscious and specific, had they taken the trouble to do precise calculations: reconstruct the dates of, for instance, whatever vacation trip was in question, and then determined how old I had in fact been at the time before assessing the reliability of my recollections. Rather it was this systematic dismissal of potential remembrance that I found so frustrating and painful.

For I knew that my own images were intense, vivid, and in some way accurate, if not by reality's yardstick, then by some other less secular measure, and I yearned for confirmation to legitimize what was to me more tangible than the brick and wood of our house, the green blades of the backyard, or the flesh and blood we all, at least partly, are.

when it is time I start kindergarten. I like it after a few days when it is not so new anymore even though the first day I cried until mama came to take me home. then it is fine she is right I get used to it but in the middle of the year we move to a house more far out on the fancy road and mama has to drive me to school every day back to near the big brick building where now we don't live anymore. doing that makes me tired and I think it makes her tired too. then she gets a city job which we were closer to before. I don't understand it seems silly to me but papa says that is where all the jobs are and that people drive much more far than our new green sign to work everyday then come all the way back.

now that mama works like papa she is really too tired to take me and pick me up at school so now I have to take two buses and walk six blocks to get home six because the second bus passes by our new house and the bus driver says he can't stop before the place he is supposed to stop he's not allowed and I wonder why we had to move.

when I ask why we needed a house papa tells me so granny can move in because she is too old to take care of herself she has falled down too many times and because of the falls she has pins in her hip. even with a cane it is hard for her to get places and the bones don't get stronger again so easy not like mine could. how would it look if I could see through her clothes and skin? like a safety pin connecting the skeleton parts? or like a whole forest of sharp roots stuck into a pin cushion that isn't soft?

A feather is an astonishingly elaborate and specialized product of the epidermis of a bird, and it is made of practically nothing but keratin, certain of the keratinized cells in this case sticking firmly together, instead of falling apart, because of a special bonding of the keratin between adjacent cells. Keratin is a very strong substance, and the form of the feather is mechanically extremely sound. The result is a wonderfully light and very efficient structure.

don't bother granny they say so I don't even though I don't like being all alone in the big house. I only visit if she calls me then we play old maid or hearts and she teaches me solitaire. granny says it is good to know a game you can play alone and

52

sometimes we play side by side. she gives me money when I win at cards or sometimes for no reason but mama makes me give it back. she says that is why I have allowance so I can buy candy and things. I heard her and papa fighting over how much it should be.

The barbs which together make up the vane on each side of the central spine or rachis, are each provided with barbules (radii). The hooked distal barbules of each barb catch upon the curved proximal barbules of each (like long pointed spoons) of the next barb (barb next more distal) and thus constitute the continuous looking vane (vexillyum). If they come unhooked by accident, they can be made to engage again by stroking the feather from base to tip as done by the bird in the act of preening . . .

I go to the grocery store with my mama which is boring but I like sitting in the cart even though she says I am really too big to sit in it now but she does like when I help her carry the bags into the house except I can only carry one at a time. but after I fall and chip my tooth on the handle of the cart in the store she always says no no absolutely not whenever I ask to sit and be pushed she won't even let me push it. you walk beside me she says hold my hand and that is even more boring.

we come home from groceries and find granny falled on the floor her cane past where she can reach. my mama gets upset. I would be upset too except granny says I am alright I've only fallen help me up now please.

I ask mama can't I stay home to take care of granny while she does groceries to play cards instead of buying the boring food and things and looking down every row where what we need is hiding but mama says no so I don't ask again. sometimes I think mama might rather be back in apartment too all squished us three when there wasn't so much to do and take care of and we didn't have room for everyone.

The sternum or breast-bone has a well-developed keel (carina) in modern flying birds (carinates) which gives attachment to the strong pectoral muscles and greatly strengthens the whole bone.

even though school year is almost over I switch to a more near school. this will be easier now mama says for you and me Clara. and even though I like better having only one bus to take I think it might have been easier to wait until the beginning of next school year.

but mama and papa both say this way you will be used to it by then you'll be glad you did it. still I don't understand where anything is bells ring all the time everybody is running trying to find their rooms. there are so many people and nobody knows who I am. the teachers don't notice me except to ask if I am lost I look lost they say but to me everybody looks that way only difference is they all find their rooms and I am always late. the teachers are not surprised after a while just nod their head. I know my cousin laura is here too she is a grade ahead of me but it is hard to find anyone with all the people.

taking just one bus home is the easiest part. in a week I learn the way back by heart so I can walk if I want to. that is nicer and not very far. when I get home there is still some time before mama gets home so I lie in my room a much bigger one than my old room it always feels so big and cold. I lie in the bed and close my eyes and try to feel very large like in a dream. I shut them tight and try to press my smallness out.

at night it is harder not to feel small and like the room swallowed a tiny me a room big enough to have two closets on each side so before I go to bed I open them one two tiptoeing between to check that no robber or monster is inside and even after I'm tucked in even if it's mama who tucks me I still think maybe somebody is there.

if I am so scared I can't sleep I read a book. it is very good to do it at the scary times since mama and papa's room is down-stairs here and it would be scary to go get them through so much dark space, scarier than somebody in the closet or bad dreams or a spider.

The two clavicles are fused together in the mid-line forming the furcula ("wishbone" or "merry though"). The angle of the furcula is generally widest in birds with strong flight, the bone acting as a curved strut to brace the wings apart. It is said that a bird cannot fly if one side of the furcula is broken . . .

Every Thursday was traumatic for me because the entire court of not peer but blood jury ruled against me and condoned their collective thievery. I tried time after time to merge my view of history with their long-standing gospel, never able to understand why my additions or alterations were shunned, not serious enough to constitute blasphemy.

As a result, yes, I am fairly certain of this causality, I decided, even young as I then was, to devote myself to the study of the natural sciences. It was not quite a conscious decision on my part, and I was too young then to understand the direct correlation that wisdom of maturity now affords me: how the resolve provided factual foundation, inviolate against them, to compensate for my failure to achieve participation through the more subjective ele-ment called memory.

it's hard to be mixed up all the time the last part of the school year but I get to know things better and feel a little bit less lost. when summer comes everything is quiet and easy even though I feel lonesome. I don't have to go anywhere except when we go to the cabin in the woods just us three. mama and papa take off work and aunt jean stays with granny and it is small and cozy in the cabin like the apartment was and that is so fun and nice to be together just us three again. papa cooks outside. the water is cold. when the sun is gone there is no light except from our lantern but the dark is not scary dark here it is fun dark.

when school starts again I tell mama she was right it is easier now I'm glad it is not new and I already know. fine fine didn't I tell you but after the first week there is a meeting and it turns out I wasn't the only one mixed up there was a mix up with the grown ups too because they put me in the wrong grade ahead of what I was supposed to and mama says I could not have made that mistake but the teachers tell her I am smart enough. but mama says Clara was going from room to room the chaos that is too much for a kindergarten age child. later she asks me why didn't you tell us it seemed different? don't yell at me mama I say I didn't know what it was supposed to and she says yes yes of course and says she is sorry and cries a little but she is always worried for a long time after.

because she is worried so easy I try to do everything right not say anything just go to school and back every day and not make noise when I'm home. I like school so much better because since they let me stay a grade ahead I am in the same class with laura. this makes me not mind the bad things but I don't think I should tell mama because she might worry I won't pay attention to the teacher. I do most of the time we only look at each other a lot and sometimes write notes we don't giggle in class. at home I even straighten my room but not as many times as I do granny's. I sneak in when mama is at work still or busy because she says I shouldn't make granny tired. but I know granny is lonesome and that is what makes her feel so tired she told me so.

in spring time when I see flowers peeking out of the ground on my way home from school my mama tells me I will have a sister or brother soon. I don't need one I think since laura is like a sister and why do they need someone besides me? so I tell mama I don't want one give it back. she says they can't do that now and I must be vestibule. it will be fun she says having a sister or brother it will cheer me up but already she spends so much

*time fixing up the extra room calls it nursery now and almost
never tells me bedtime stories she sends papa instead.*

*his stories are OK too it isn't really that it is more that she
is already so busy and tired how will she have somebody extra
around too? I tell her she can leave it in the big city and see it
when she goes to work. she laughs and says no that would be
bad for baby it will live here with us and probably she will stop
the job. wouldn't I like her around more?*

We received only a smattering of this discipline in school,
and I spent increasingly long sessions in the school library after
classes were over, eventually supplementing those resources with
the public library's and finally with the special collections of
university libraries.

I loved this new information, as did my parents and teachers,
and my mother was only too pleased to chauffeur me to these
sites in order to facilitate my research. The librarian informed me
that I was the youngest student on record to use interlibrary loan.
This option was particularly useful when I came to need more
specialized texts.

I did sense, after a several-year period, the adults found my
hobby somewhat disconcerting: frightening in quantity of research and seriousness of application. Nonetheless, during its initial stages, the project lent me the validity I sorely needed; for
if I presented my mother with information about mating habits,
gestation period and respiratory structures of bird, fish or insect,
she would more than likely say, "Isn't that interesting Clara," rather
than challenge me on the subject, quibbling over the technicalities
of sound repetition in bird vocalization, or debating whether
double circulation is a feature ascribed to mammal or fish. She
had no investment in that information; thus it did not constitute
a threat.

*for my eighth birthday I get a puppy. I'm glad they got me
something that has nothing to do with the house like the new*

bedroom set when we first moved or the piano lessons I didn't want last year. puppy is friendly and funny and I take him outside on walks but sometimes he goes to the bathroom on the grass and the neighbors get mad. right on the lawn oh please says the lady who is always guarding her rose bushes when we go by. when the lady is inside her house which is almost never I pick a white rose to put in the vase in granny's room. granny likes a rose but mama would say it is not responsible.

responsible is using the tool they got me to clean up after puppy. papa says we have to use it in this town but I think it is silly and gross so I leave it against the garage door before I start to walk puppy and fetch it on the way back. I think they got me puppy so I could have a sort of baby too and wouldn't mind when theirs comes but it isn't working that way.

I wish I could give puppy right back because I like it better when laura and me go into the woods after school to eat berries even though her mother and mine told us to never eat wild things because they might be poison. but we decide that if we die we will die together and the vultures will eat us.

we are both scared but it is fun. if we don't feel like doing something scary we sit in the parking lot a few blocks from school near the dumpster that says DO NOT PLAY ON OR AROUND and we watch the birds fly away all together their tails like seashells in the sky. then we walk home stopping at her house first or mine if we go the long way around. I can stay out till dark on the days I don't have chores listed under my name on the refrigerator and those are my favorite days.

Feathers, the bird's most distinctive and remarkable acquisition, are magnificently adapted for fanning the air, for insulation against the weather and for reduction of weight. It has been claimed that for their weight they are stronger than any wing structure devised by man. Their flexibility allows the broad trailing edge of each large wing-feather to bend upward with each downstroke of the wing.

This produces the equivalent of pitch in a propeller plane, so that each wingbeat provides both lift and forward propulsion. When a bird is landing or taking off, its strong wingbeats separate the large primary wing feathers at their tips, thus forming wing-slots which help prevent stalling. It seems remarkable that man took so long to learn some of the fundamentals of airplane design that even the lowliest of English sparrows demonstrates to perfection.

Once my goal was established, the work before me and the dedication required to fulfill it were clear. Each day, systematically, I tried to correct my allegedly invalid perceptions: to redeem them by way of the empirical. At first I was more intrigued by the research itself than by the living specimens which were its subject, though when my path crossed the designated creatures I would take note of and delight in their characteristics, unique qualities: form. Yet I loved the language of my ever-accumulating reference material, which my fellow classmates found arid, tedious and too specialized to be within the domain of their youthful comprehension.

For me these creatures, and any mention or description of them, was mysterious, magical; I never ceased to be in awe of their intricacies, also covetous of them, for it seemed that those intricacies, unlike human ones, were intelligently designed, to their advantage and expediency, and what's more, unity; rather than to their befuddlement and exasperation. Psychological nuance did not have a chance to interfere with perfection.

Development is a simple and straightforward matter when one considers mother bird teaching offspring to fly, nourishing it with food from her beak, until such time that it can find its own food, and fly from the nest she warms it in. Then, when it is on its own, there are no confusions. The break is clean; independence is clarity. Though thrust into what might be perceived as a brutal environment, i.e., nature, the fledgling's circumstance is also characterized by—and we would be imperceptive, even unjust not to acknowledge—a purity, a precision, that contrasts (quite favorably to my mind) with the murky set of variables wrought by that complex phenomenon we call personality.

granny is not in her room when I get home. when I ask papa he says she has a different room for a while at the hospital. who took her away I ask him. he says they came for her in the ambulance but only because it is easier not because it was an emergency. can I visit her in the hospital I ask him. granny will be back very soon he says she is having an operation to make her better. he and mama don't seem worried so I think he must be right I should believe him.

one day I come home early because laura was sick with a cold and couldn't play, and I hear someone crying then I figure out it is mama. she is home early and papa is there too everyone is home when they aren't supposed to be but I don't disturb them behind the closed bedroom door. granny must be very worse to make mama cry I think and when papa comes to my room I know what he will tell me.

but he surprises me. the bad news is different he tells me I will not have a brother or sister after all not now anyway and that makes me feel better about granny. I don't ever tell him the things I feel but he looks at me funny and says I know you are sad about this Clara which means it would be wrong not to feel sad.

I was attracted to the idea of behavior induced by instinct: how utterly simple. That messy issue of motivation replaced by drives which create a natural community rather than fragmentation and chaos. To fly together, to migrate, to breed, nourish, sing. How perfectly adapted they were to environment, in one respect like small perfect machines; and yet magical, in that they were not bound to earth, possessing a completely different medium to which they were ideally suited.

* * *

that summer laura and I are sent to camp together which
makes me mind less than if I had to go alone. in some ways it is
harder than school even though there is no work only play because
you have to stay for a whole month sometimes two and be with
other children all the time. you can't make up your own games
you have to play dumb ones already made up and sleep on cots
in one room and use water that is cold and smells like rotten
eggs. there are lots and lots of bugs. they have two toilets in the
same bathroom and you aren't supposed to lock the door.

everyone changes into their bathing suits together to go
swimming no gym lockers like at school. the counselors put on
their bathing suits with the campers. for the first time I see an
older girl her different body things that have happened to it. later
in the cafeteria I eat bread and butter and it reminds me of her
body when I spread the smooth yellow on the soft white I don't
know why. it bothers me I keep thinking of it. laura is not like
that but she will be before I am. I don't want her to be or me to
be.

Particularly interesting cases of female song are those
in which it occurs as duetting; that is, when two members
of a pair sing simultaneously as part of the courtship display
or to maintain the pair bond. . . . In a number of South
American tyrant-flycatchers . . . a very special duetting known
as antiphonal singing occurs. In this type, two members of
a pair may alternate with extraordinarily accurate timing,
often singing different phrases, so that unless one is actually
watching it may be impossible to tell that the song is not
coming from one bird.

uncle arthur picks us up at camp and we don't even mind
how long the drive is because we are glad to be going home. but
when I get in the house mama and papa look very serious. they

didn't tell me because they didn't want to upset me spoil my fun at camp and they decided I was too young to go to a sad thing like a funeral. granny must have been so lonesome at the hospital with no one to talk to or play cards with unless the nurses did. I bet she thought I left her all alone. I can't feel happy for more than two years and mama and papa say something must be wrong with me they want to send me to some doctor.

We spend our whole lives, don't we, living out that legacy, challenging and fulfilling an upbringing with which we have a thousand quarrels, griefs and grudges we harbor inside? But then, if they be put to the test, if we take up these bones with our past persecutors whom we have never been able to shake from that stone barring our tomb we call memory, there are disputes; there is no hope of verification, so that it might seem ludicrous to accuse the very ones who gave us life, for our present difficulties, even incapacities and debilities. If I were, for instance, utterly lacking in love and compassion, emotional growth stunted to the degree of being crippled, and I, at the witness stand assert this, mother or father are sure to refute with visceral testimony: she whom I carried in my womb, whom I healed so many times from every infant malady. She claims I stole, when the truth is I sold my own soul in order to create her. How easily, and irrefutably they can dismiss your case.

it is much later when laura and me are walking home from school looking at the leaves turning pretty colors that she tells me something happened to make her different. I almost forgot about that thinking of granny and other things. laura says she's not supposed to tell me but she wants me to be ready because someday I'll be different too and she can't stand to have a secret from me anyway. usually it is me explaining something to laura that she doesn't understand. she says she is not allowed to tell exactly what except that it happens to everyone who is a girl and I spend weeks imagining what the horrible thing will be to make

*me into bread and butter. I'll be sick and everyone will know but
no one will talk about it. will it hurt I ask laura. she says it does
but not the way you'd expect. nights I dream of birds pecking
me apart in the woods or a slow poison from inside my body not
caused by any berry.*

My parents were, for quite some time, pleased and supportive; I believe they felt a particular pride in me: the child whom
they had begun to fear a lost cause, and who was now, at last,
excelling at something. Mastery did not come about all at once
by any means; I did, however, manage very gradually to accrue
a staggering amount of knowledge. At times my own ability surprised me. I suppose I had, as people say, a "feel" for it.

Indeed, I cherished the books on my shelves, which had a
high turnover rate, my reading so voracious that one thick volume
substituted for its successor within a matter of days. A few were
constants: those my reference bibles. I felt no guilt, as I was not
explicitly aware of this pastime's function as defense against my
parents, who now praised me as I trotted off on Thursday evenings
to the library, no longer envious of their gatherings.

Anxiety replaced their pride as they observed my hobby
become something closer to obsession: a singular preoccupation
which precluded almost all ordinary child-activities, the very
things which bring one to the threshold of young adulthood. I
was not, to their mind, becoming "socialized"; I seemed to have
radically decreasing interest in and tolerance for anything outside
the realm of natural science; remaining a very selective bibliophile
who spent little time dialoguing with nature "in vivo" as it were.

Let me summarize. The physiology and acoustics of
bird vocalization are unique in the animal kingdom. Sound
is produced at the syrinx in the air stream modulated by an
elastic membrane vibrating in a restricted passage bounded
by the walls of the bronchus. This source-generated acoust-
ical disturbance appears not to be modified in its passage

through the trachea. The syrinx contains two independently controllable sources, one in each bronchus, enabling the bird to produce two notes or phrases simultaneously. Harmonics arise below a threshold frequency by mechanical constraints on the vibrating membrane, forcing a departure from the purely sinusoidal wave form. The source-generated sounds can be modulated in frequency or amplitude or (more usually) in both with extraordinary rapidity, so rapidly that human ears cannot perceive the modulators as such, receiving instead impressions of notes of varying quality or timbre.

I can't stand it anymore not knowing so tell my mother I was just wondering not because anyone said anything to me but I have a feeling something will happen to me soon and does she know anything about this? my mother tells me it is too early to think about things I can't understand yet and makes me tell her what started me wondering.

this is the last I see of my cousin for a long time. I made a big mistake. she is not allowed to come over after school and the teacher puts us in separate classes. when mama finds out we were in the same class all this time she is mad at me too and now we are both in trouble. we are not supposed to be together at lunch or even recess. that seems like a lot for just telling one secret. I hope laura is not being punished in any other way I don't know about. I feel bad I had to tell who told me. I was dumb and not brave at all. and still I don't know what will happen to me that no one will tell but now I am sure it will be worse than it would have been though I don't think I'll even know that it's happening when it does I won't be able to ask laura if it is the thing.

The first time was in fact the last my parents were courteous about their wish to broaden my interests and activities. Had I not resisted, who knows how the events of my youth and adolescence would have proceeded, what course my life would have taken.

Yet I did resist, with all my will, for I felt and felt deeply that they were trying, again, to rob me, of the only thing I possessed; they had no business interfering, no true understanding or appreciation.

I wanted to surrender no increment of time I spent with my precious books, my studies. How easy it would have been to compromise: consent to weekly lessons, occasional parties. Never mind diligent practice at home or enthusiasm; mere attendance might have satisfied them. It was not so much to ask. But a child is not equipped to formulate compromises, and I was a particularly stubborn specimen of my species.

I would have none of their extracurricular activities, which seemed trivial, silly compared to my own elevated pursuits. Hadn't they once praised me? Hadn't my teachers also done so? But as far as my parents were concerned at this point, their daughter's new hobby was excess.

> . . . When a bird undertakes to sing, it in effect closes a valve between the lung and the syrinx. Then it compresses (with its chest muscles) the air in a system of sacs. Pressure in the clavicular sac, which surrounds the syrinx, forces the exceedingly thin tympanic membrane into the bronchial passage, closing it momentarily. . . . Tension is then applied to the syringeal muscles, which, acting in opposition to the sac pressure, withdraw the bulged membrane from the opposite bronchial wall, thus creating a passage through the bronchial tube. Air streaming through the passage past the tensed membrane stimulates it to vibrate, and song is produced . . .

On Tuesday evening of the following week, my mother came to the library, as usual, at closing time, to fetch me home. It was her practice to wait in the parked car directly in front of the entryway, both of us punctual—I would come out to her rather than she in to me—especially since the strain of their incipient disapproval now put me in a particularly awkward position, dependent as I was upon her generosity for transportation.

But this Tuesday I found her in the vestibule instead of the car, thought little of the variation, but inquired, merely curious. She told me she'd been early and hadn't cared to wait in the car. As to the shopping bag under her arm, she said she had thought there was a waste can inside, for she'd spent the first few minutes since arriving cleaning the interior of the car.

Reasonable enough, I thought, but after our silent ride home, I realized I'd been lied to, and worse, robbed again: all my library books, I discovered, had been removed with no substitutes, returned without my permission. All I had left were my text books for school: English, Social Studies, Science, Math. My parents had confiscated even my reference books. This was indeed coercion.

So in answer to my having refused to give an inch, they had taken a mile, and I would never gain any of that measure back, not while I lived in their house, and precious few other prospects did I have as an eleven-year-old, save running away, which was as reckless as it was obvious, too melodramatic and unoriginal for my taste. When I had collected myself, I schemed.

then the thing happens. my mother is more helpful than I thought she would be she gives me instruction and says she didn't expect it to happen so soon. the other time when I thought she had come to tell me she just told me about adam and eve a story I already knew. she told me when I was sick with a bad cold lying in bed with the vaporizer on which is when I first guessed the change must be some kind of sickness.

when will it go away I ask her now and she says soon but later she tells me it keeps coming back almost forever till I'm older than she is. like having a flu on schedule I think so you can plan it and worry. can I go to the bathroom I ask her and she says of course don't be ridiculous but I'm still not sure. if only I knew how long it would last I would be able to know if I could hold out. don't take a bath though she says and disappears to speak to papa. I don't want him to know about my sickness why does she have to tell him?

    ... The fact is that the rapid modulations we have been discussing cannot be perceived as such by human ears ... It is easy for us to resolve a trill or tremolo if its frequency is thirty cycles per second or less, but when the frequency rises to one hundred cycles per second or more we hear a note of a rather unpleasant buzzy quality. Hence the beautiful complexity of the lapland longspur is completely lost in our ears, whereas it seems more than likely that Madame Longspur finds it delightful and enticing.

I was genuinely distraught, felt I no longer had identity, after such assiduous labor to attain one. Now that I had no access to the information which had become my daily bread—for I knew that any attempt to regain the books would be as futile as asking them to accept my memories as valid—I required a substitute, even if a vastly inferior one. It would not have occurred to me at that time to seek a source within myself, and so I turned in desperation to the only remaining external sources, which had previously seemed inadequate at best: my school books. I found that literature and mythology, subjects which had hitherto eluded me, were full of reverence for my special friends. This language was much harder to decode than that of fact: what I was accustomed to. But I became engrossed, immersing myself, lingering over lines such as this: "My heart in hiding/Stirred for a bird, ... And the fire that breaks from thee then, a billion/Times told lovelier, more dangerous ... and blue-bleak embers, ah my dear,/ Fall, gall themselves, and gash gold-vermillion." As my new passion was not on the surface, subversive, it was as good as invisible, and thus truly inviolate, affording me rebellion in the guise of acquiescence.

now I do so well in school that the teachers call in my mama and papa they all have a meeting while I wait outside. they decide I should transfer to a different school a school I will also live at. I am sure this is a punishment in disguise. I should have done poorly in school instead.

just when I am used to the place I have to leave but what difference does it make anyway without laura? I may as well be far away. I think mama and papa will be glad to be rid of me.

I don't cry on the day I leave. I got all my crying done the night before in my room where no one can hear. I'm surprised mama cries as she waves goodbye. she doesn't come along in the car with papa. I don't feel like talking to him so I sit in the back seat pretend he's the chauffeur.

Dear Clara,

I'm so sad they sent you away to school, but I figured out it's not as bad as not being able to see you here because at least I can write to you now, since your mother won't know. She came over here after your Dad drove you up. She was kind of upset. I eavesdropped as much as I could. She was here a long time. All she said was she wanted to do what was best for you, she said it about twenty times, I think. Even my Mom says your Mom is a little funny sometimes. Extreme is the word she uses. But Mom got her calmed down before she left. I'll let you know everything that happens. So much has happened to me in the last couple of months, but I'll tell you all about that in the next letter. I'll try to write every few days. Don't be too lonely, Clar. Maybe I can even sneak up and visit sometime.

Your faithful cousin,
Laura

the boarding school is near woods pretty I like that but don't like having to live with two other girls who don't I'm positive like having to share their room with someone new. they are used to just the two of them. they whisper to each other after the lights are out and I hear them like insects buzzing across the room.

I like to do the homework because it takes up so much time and gives me reason to be in the library away. I get excellent grades since I study a lot especially english. while all the girls are reading gushy shakespeare sonnets I do extra credit projects on much harder poems like the one called the phoenix and the turtle. the teacher said she didn't understand everything in my paper but that she could tell it was very smart. no one else talks to me except behind my back I think they talk about me.

I don't go to meals because I think they are doing that whenever I see them whispering in groups and I don't want to have to talk to anyone anyway in that huge room with so many tables where everyone is talking about something even if it isn't me because they've known each other so long. the library is nice and quiet during meal times I like being there I'm hardly ever hungry anymore. and what is better is the thing stopped way before mama said it would. wait till she hears how lucky I am she will be surprised.

COLOUR: in birds, especially that of the feathers (SEE FEATHER: PLUMAGE). The colours are due to some but not all the components of the incident white light. When all the components of white light are reflected the bird will appear to be white. There are two ways in which colours can be removed from the incident white light a) by the physical nature of the reflecting surface, to give structural colours; and b) by certain chemical attributes, to give pigmentary colours. Some colours are due to a combination of these two methods. The removal of some parts of the spectrum by these methods results in the reflection of the remaining parts.

it's me who's surprised to see my mother at school they must have asked her to come after they sent for the doctor. they didn't need to do either of those. I feel ok. or maybe mama sent the doctor. she gets hysterical as soon as she sees me. you are pitifully thin she says I had no idea then screams why did you stop eating. calm down mama I say not in front of the headmaster but mama won't calm down not until I let her take me to the doctor at home too to be looked at again. this doctor tells me everything will be alright but I have to go to all the meals even if I'm busy or not hungry and he will see me again when I come home for vacation. then he and mama talk while I wait outside.

I can't hear through the door except a long latin word I don't understand the name of my not eating. I love not having the thing anymore but mama is still upset. all the way back to school from the doctor's she is yelling at me why why as if it were a sickness that I cured myself.

Dear Clara,

Your Mom was really off the deep end this time. I hope she didn't make problems up there. I'm sure you don't really look like a skeleton. Mom says she does exaggerate. But were you really doing that other neat stuff—jumping out of trees and weird lab experiments, making them let you take physics with the much older students? Unless Aunt Celia made it up. Remember when we used to play at the dumpster? That must seem like kid stuff to you now. It was kind of hard not to laugh when your mother kept saying, "And why couldn't she just go to gym class and use the trampoline instead like all the other girls?" But you know, Clara, you can't stay a tomboy forever. The guys don't really like it even though they act like they do. I know because I have a sort of boyfriend now. His name is Jerry and I'm

sending you a picture of him. Isn't he cute? What are the
boys like at that fancy school? Do you girls get to see much
of them? I have to go meet Jerry now, but I'll write again
soon. You better write back too, or I'll get mad. No, really,
I'll go nuts unless I hear from you. And Clara, this is the
best, I volunteered to help you get normal again, so that
when you come home for vacation, your Mom will think
it's O.K. for us to see each other. Wasn't that smart? But
write before that, O.K.? And tell me what you think of Jerry.

Your faithful cousin,
Laura

A most peculiar entity is puberty: that universal, "natural"
rite of passage, characterized exclusively by increases, prolifera-
tions: that which can be measured. Great emphasis is placed on
growth, and nature's metaphors superimposed make rather awkward fit. One speaks of blossomings, sproutings, as if the body
were emerging from the ground in its own mimic of springtime,
that will not, alas, become cyclic; simply serve as single transition.
What is for our flora and fauna a given becomes for us self-con-
sciousness: uneasy blend of boastfulness and shame.
One kind of growing, in this paradigm, has value or validity;
one circumscribed set of changes. Any deviation is automatically
perceived as aberration; hence delinquent behavior. No one—
certainly no parent—would ever think to interpret arrested
growth as statement of some other kind of motion. Yet how
important for development of one's own self is the way we grow
away from one another, declare ourselves other, apart, so as to
have the means to craft within ourselves our own identity.

when I come home for thanksgiving break not long after my
mother's visit they say they have a surprise for me at dinner. some
special food I think they are always trying to get me to eat but
holidays usually have special food. then laura comes in from the
next room. laura. aren't you happy to see your cousin they ask

71

*but I hardly recognize her wearing a fancy dress her hair all styled
wearing makeup even. I'm surprised aunt jean would let her. it's
hard to talk with all the relatives around and everyone eating and
making me eat.*

*after dinner laura says come on let's go off by ourselves it's
been so long. you look different I say and she laughs says she
will show me how to look that way too. even though I never
wrote her back. we'll start with this she says and opens her purse
takes out makeup and puts a creamy stick of color all around her
mouth. this is good practice she says and when I ask what for
she says kissing you dummy of course.*

*so what did you think of that picture of jerry? when I shrug
my shoulders laura makes a huge sigh just like mama and then
looks bored and asks me what kinds of things do I learn at the
new place. I open a text book to show her but she takes it away
and flips through the pages very fast. while she is flipping she finds
what I forgot I did jerry's head cut from the picture she sent
pasted on top of a baboon's body. how could you clara laura says
and throws the book against the wall you are such a baby sometimes. she runs out and slams the door.*

STRUCTURAL COLOURS: those of birds are due
either to interference; giving iridescent colours that change
with the angle of view, as in soap bubbles, or to the scattering
of light, giving non-iridescent structural colours. The structure responsible for iridescence is present in barbules that
are flattened for part of their length and twisted at right angles
so that one of the flat sides comes to face the observer. This
torsion of barbules is accompanied by loss of hooklets and
flanges; this reduces the mechanical strength of the vane, and
so fully iridescent colours are not found in flight feathers . . .

Air had always seemed to me the most compelling medium:
ethereal, open, vast; that which would render me massless, and
liberate from those limiting increments one must, on ground,

proceed by. One foot in front of the other, as the saying goes: step by step. Ah, how like the psychology of the human mind, never able to bypass the plodding, point-by-point progress of the ratiocinative; whereas they, *they* are not encumbered; for them there is no issue, with no developed brain to hinder span of form. They leave the ground to sweep through sky in all the time it takes for us to blink our human, far less "seeing" eye.

I would rather go back to the school with all the girls whose difference is one sameness than be here with different laura who has turned the same as them. but I can't go back to school mama tells me no matter how good the grades are. a hundred A's she says can't make up for behavior. she calls it asocial obstructive self-destructive behavior. look up those words she says look them up in a people book. then she cries says she is sorry. papa comes in says don't be so hard on the child but frowns at me too. will she ever grow up to be normal I hear through the closed bedroom door.

It is understatement to claim that my parents were no longer pleased with me. Their approval had been fleeting, now spent. All relationships, be they past, present or future—my grandmother, passed away; my cousin, once the closest human to my heart; my parents, who might have in some different circumstance been close to me, available; and the potential peers, communication with whom was destined to be unrealized—were reduced to alienation. Irreconcilable alienation. Only in reading and in dream did I find solace. And the more the imagery of literature yielded to my labors, the richer my dreams became, sometimes themselves the equivalent of poem or myth. These realms, exclusively, held hope: a glimpse of liberation.

The most famous and poetic of all fabulous birds is the Phoenix. Pliny describes it as being the size of an eagle, with a gold neck, purple body, azure tail, and crested head

. . . There was said to be only one Phoenix in the world at a time, and it dwelt in Paradise, a land of infinite beauty beyond the eastern horizon. Every thousand years, the Phoenix left paradise and flew westwards to die. It collected aromatic plants on the way from the spice groves of Arabia, and built itself a nest in the top of a tall palm tree. Here on the first dawn after its journey, it sang a song of such surpassing beauty that the sun-god stopped in his chariot to listen. When he whipped up his horses again, sparks from the hooves set fire to the nest of the Phoenix, and it died on a blazing aromatic funeral pyre. The new Phoenix grew from a worm which was found in the ashes of the nest and flew back to Paradise for its own allotted lifespan of a thousand years.

And now we must alter our perspective. This mode of telling is no longer adequate, for the events which follow are of a different order from all which have been recorded until this point. Let us consider, for example, the information we have just received: the same information that the child, Clara, has received. It is a passage from a reference book, is it not? And yet we know Clara no longer has access to her reference books. This is a trick, you think, to see if you have been paying attention. You have followed the plot, and you know that Clara has had free access to the library at boarding school; all libraries house reference books. But you also know that the girl has been resourceful; you probably sense that she is on a journey toward sources more primary than those texts with which she was preoccupied through puberty.

We might ask a simple question: does she need such information anymore? The girl herself would insist she does; that she has in fact been changed by the picture these words have painted. Let us then modify our question. Does Clara require any longer this particular mode of presentation? Ah, you say, that is another matter. It may well be the case that such a presentation cannot do justice to the images at stake, and thus be incomplete, or even false.

Let us imagine then—or rather, assume—that Clara has dreamt this piece of text, which has been transformed into image; become, as it were, animate. The child's sleep is understandably restless; for the dream has, in one sense, awakened her, prepared her for the journey she must take, although she does not have— at least not until this moment—the means, the wherewithal to make it, as the movement required is far more esoteric, more elaborate than that of eyes across a page.

The girl, who has experienced profound isolation and sadness, loneliness, is now also deeply afraid. She has done, as we know, a good deal of preparation. But thorough and systematic application cannot assist her through the final stages of this process, for which no child could be prepared. And in many ways, despite her difference, Clara has been, until this point, an ordinary girl. Not average; we would not call her average. But not extraordinary either. Precocious, sensitive: these are the words one might, objectively, use. The child, meanwhile, feels far removed from any useful perspective on the separateness she so keenly feels.

ENTER MOTHER.

[She stoops to kiss the sleeping child, lingers in that posture, as if she might have some special access to her daughter in the vulnerable state of sleep, as if she might be able to inspect what images inhabit the girl's subconscious. Or perhaps she merely craves the intimacy, seeks solace; as her own nocturnal hours have been eventful also. It is time we allowed Clara's mother her own voice.]

MOTHER: Clara. Clara, dear. I'm sorry to wake you, sweetheart, but I couldn't wait until morning. There's something I want to tell you. I had a wonderful idea.

[The child's eyes open, blink. She appears puzzled. Is she trembling?]

Now don't worry, I didn't come to yell. Mama isn't such an ogre she would wake up her Clara to yell at her. I'm sorry about losing my temper before. You musn't mind when Mama does that. The problem is—and this is why I want to chat, dear—we sent you too far away for school, and all the while I could have been showing you so many useful things at home. We don't need to send you back to that boarding school. I wish I'd thought of it before. We can get re-acquainted, and you can ask me any questions, tell me the things that confuse you, and you won't feel so much by yourself anymore. You can even see your cousin again. Wouldn't you like that? That's been the trouble, hasn't it?

[The child cannot yet reply, for she is overwhelmed with imagery, on the edge of consciousness. Inside her mind are fireworks, shooting stars: a catalogue of flame. A forest's green goes red, then black and from that dark emerges a young woman leading an army, triumphant. Then she is vanquished; men make a pyre of her flesh, as she raises her eyes toward heaven, and suddenly her body becomes hundreds of bodies; a blue flame takes their collective breath; they are ash, and finally a vast dark ominous cloud shaped like something that comes from the earth burns all traces of life.]

MOTHER: Darling, you're shivering. You must be cold. [she puts her palm against the child's forehead] No, you're warm, I think, quite warm. Our Clara wouldn't have a fever, would she? That's what comes from not eating enough; you have no resistance. I think what you need is a nice big breakfast, and that can be our first lesson. Mama will show you how to cook and we can chat in the kitchen. Come along, then, Miss Sleepyhead. [the child extends her hand, remains supine] You want to be carried, is that it? Well, all right. Mama can carry this feather-girl. [the two descend slowly down the stairs, the girl in the woman's arms] I know my daughter well enough to know she'd just as soon not have her feet on the ground. But soon everything will be different, Clara. You'll feel confident, like

76

your cousin, like any normal girl your age. And I'll teach you everything. Then before you know it you'll be all grown up with a husband and you'll want a baby and then your friend will stop for the right reason. Nature will work in you to make a change instead of you tampering with it. You see, dear, that's the wonderful thing: everything has its own natural pattern and all you need is not to interfere. I probably didn't explain enough during our chat—remember when Mama told you about Adam and Eve and the rest? We haven't had enough chats; that's the problem. We'll fix that now.

[They have reached the kitchen, and the mother sits her daughter at the table while she goes to light the stove.]

You'll be a wonderful cook by that time. Do you remember, back in the apartment, before we moved, how you used to love watching me cook? We spent so much time in the kitchen. But now I can't make up my mind what to teach you first. I want to show you how to knit, too, because there's nothing nicer than knitting while you watch the baby in your tummy grow bigger and bigger. And knowing how to mend is very practical, of course. Laura could come over for sewing lessons with you, if you'd like that, though she seems much more interested in buying clothes from what your aunt reports. Let me run upstairs and get the yarn and needles anyway; we'll try a little bit of everything. You go ahead and light the stove then, dear, so things are nice and cozy for us. That's the first step for any cooking or baking, after all. You're grown up enough to be trusted not to play with matches.

[The mother hands the box of kitchen matches to her daughter, and hurries up the stairs.]

Clara longs to show her mother a stitching more compelling than the frail fabric of human crafting: threads with which we tie our lives together. But the girl's mother, in her ardent efforts to initiate her daughter into domestic ritual and train her for fulfillment and integration, would likely only crush the unlovely segmented body that is the secret of time's suture. And how, in any case, would the child communicate her longing? The voice to do so is not just yet in her power.

MOTHER RETURNS.

[She is greeted by fire. All about her are flames, and her daughter is nowhere in sight. She calls her name as she grabs a cannister of salt and hurls the tiny white crystals into the sea of flame.]

MOTHER: Clara, are you hiding, darling? That's a good instinct, to run from danger. But Mama will get everything under control. At least it's nice and warm now. Sometimes just before dawn feels so cold. That's part of growing up: not being bothered by life's little catastrophes, taking them in stride. You can come out now, Clara; we don't need to stop our chat. Mama has plenty of salt.

Do you remember the special doctor I tried to have you visit? The one who said you should tell me how you feel about things. I was thinking, dear, that you were right. *[she coughs a long while before continuing]* It is a bit smoky, isn't it, dear? You could do Mama a favor and open the window. But I thought to myself, Clara can tell her own Mama without some silly doctor, even if she's not used to doing that. We could sit together quietly, maybe knit; the rhythm of knitting is very relaxing. I know you'd enjoy it. I always did.

And I haven't done much of it since I was pregnant with you. I'd knit hours on end then, and feel so peaceful. I often miss that time, though I couldn't do much else: couldn't lie on my stomach or hold something in my lap. The last month I couldn't even breathe after a few bites of food—because I felt you in there, a constant heaviness, that made me want to be light, dream of it. You such a tiny thing, you can't imagine that. Did you think Mama wouldn't be able to see you if you shrunk yourself so thin? Did you think you could hide from us all so we wouldn't bother you? That's what Clara wanted, wasn't it? But of course you don't like yourself, darling, because you haven't blossomed yet. You just need some special attention and I realize I haven't been giving it until now. I know you'll be blossoming soon.

[Suddenly each arm of flame appears to take wing; a battalion of birds fly out of the fire, which would seem to have generated them.]

On Thursday evenings of the girl's childhood, one name often served as catalyst for dormant sensations, but that process was merest adumbration for this far grander fireworks, searing yet illuminating: a multitextured incendiary imagery: container for a thousand years of memory. Surely it is a richer proliferation than that which characterizes puberty when suddenly she is thirty-in-one birds.

[The mother runs out of the room and returns moments later with a fly swatter. Shoo, shoo, she cries, flailing the limp weapon.]

MOTHER: Oh, Clara. Such peculiar things are happening tonight. But you mustn't be frightened. I wish you would bring me the butterfly net Papa bought you last summer. Then I could catch these funny birds. They must have come in the chimney; it happens sometimes, like squirrels or bats. You've heard of that.

[She continues to strike at the air with the swatter; the birds neither pursue her nor flee from her.]

I do wish you'd come out of your hiding place, dear, but I know you're here somewhere—just the way I knew you were with me when I carried you all those months. Just imagine, Clara—you're so good at that, aren't you—carrying some-one up a mountain, someone who isn't very big at first.

Weight isn't what makes you notice the someone. It's more a feeling, of not being alone, of suddenly having company, but all the time. You have your arms tight around the some- one for months and months, and her weight increases as the altitude does. Up you both go, and the growing person locked in your arms so tight gets impatient too, kicks at you because both of you want to get to the top faster and have the journey over. And I can see my little someone is as obstinate as ever so that I'll have to hunt for that butterfly net all by myself without her help. *[She pauses before exiting, uncertain of whether to carry the implement with her or set it down. She does the latter.]*

And what of Clara's journey? Could she share it with her mother? Could she possibly articulate her liberation? She needn't struggle any more, the girl: not against the world's mass, as Sisyphus did, nor against pursuers as did Ovid's creatures—though her change will be akin to theirs. Nor need she wrestle with the debris of ages, as Hercules did. Soon, very soon to be realized is Clara's different and singular task: pouring forth sound into air, in articulate, rapturous flame.

[The mother returns, yet again, with an inappropriate instrument, for the creatures she battled, albeit ineffectually, are no longer visible; nor is there raging flame to contend with. A floor covered with soot is what remains. Momentarily frustrated, she tosses the net aside.]

MOTHER: Well, at least this time I know exactly what I need to use and where it is. The broom is in the kitchen, and sweeping is something your Mama is very good at. This is a good opportunity for me to show you, Clara, if you'd ever show yourself to me, because there's an art to sweeping. It seems so easy, but to do it thoroughly and well takes con- centration and practice. It's labor with a reward, and the reward is order, and so many things in life are that way, dear. Growing up is all about that: working hard and being patient. The best example is probably having a baby. For instance, when you weighed me down, loosening my firm tummy, all of me, clamoring to get out with your itty bitty, not even fully formed feet, that was still a joyous time for me, for all of us. I would say to your Papa, come here and hold your hand to this sweet bulge and feel her eagerness to join us. And your Aunt Jean had just given birth to Laura, and I'd say, put your hand here too, Jean; feel the bouncy bundle that will be a playmate for your Laura. We dreamed of the big families we would have. One big happy family, all of us.

[A worm creeps slowly across the floor, unnoticed by the mother, leaving a trail in the soot that has not yet been swept.]

Our meager human memories and fantasies and hopes weave a web of nostalgia to which we are bound; locked into compulsion through anticipation or dread, through repetition. Single events occur over and over in memory, until it seems that they concretely had repeated. How we cling to our joys and our trials; grow attached, never able to break free of the burdens we believe to be our jewels. But bonds that once seemed more than real, substantial, even immortal; when we finally see *through* them, become tenuous indeed.

What the child is becoming, however, is one whose very existence is memory: no longer Clara, no longer mere girl, but a medium for eternity. And what destiny could more completely, more perfectly meld Parmenides' stasis with Heraclitus' fire, than to be, through a transforming flame, the worm-turned-bird and bird-turned-worm who stitches all of time together?

MOTHER: Now it's your turn to sweep, Clara. Mama needs to knit a while, to calm herself. Do come out and help. *[she leans the broom against the wall, seats herself, takes up yarn and needles]*

When I pick up these needles, it all comes back to me. Everything. How it felt to be a woman swollen with love —a woman sitting in this same chair—and a hope that was hidden but burgeoning. Could I ever feel that way again, Clara? Could you let me? Could you help me? I was a tabernacle then: a house for something sacred, that was given to bring newness to my life, and Papa's life.

You tried so hard to flee us both, ever since you left the house I made myself for you. From such an early age, you were always in your room, your books, hiding from our love; forming in my belly all those months only to hide forever. Oh Clara, doesn't it seem sad to come forth only to remain unknown? My veiled child, distant child, never content to be just child, insisting on adult traits, and demanding to know what children cannot know—which reminds me of an article— Oh, dear! [she pauses, clearly alarmed] Clara, darling, I don't know how this could have happened but there are vermin in the house. And I want to make sure you understand that I always keep a clean house, to set an example for you, and because I wouldn't feel right if I didn't. But there is some dreadful thing that has intruded into our home by accident, and I am going to take this broom and make sure it goes back where it came from.

[Neither flying creature nor brutal flame could elicit the terror, the revulsion that this small crawling worm elicits. She cannot bring herself to step upon it with her slippered foot, and even making contact with it by the broom takes all her courage, so squeamish is she. As if it were some monstrous, towering adversary, she inches it back and further back until it is out of her sight.]

There, now.

[She returns to her chair after putting aside the broom. Before she takes up yarn and needles, she wipes her hands on her dressing gown.]

We won't be bothered again by that ... pest ... There
couldn't be any more of them. It never belonged here to
begin with. You really can come out now, Clara. But you'll
wait till you're good and ready; I know you. And in the
meantime, even though I'd much rather be able to see you
while we chat, I'll tell you about this article I read, in some
silly magazine. It made me think of you: how you used to
amuse us with your claims, your vivid imagination. You
weren't quite so stubborn then. But this article said that
babies may remember their own birth, or even how they
felt in the womb, before birth. Isn't that queer?

You know, Clara, lately I worry that vivid imagination
of yours is contagious, because right now I could swear I
see those birds flying straight at me, back again to haunt me,
their wings like flames, flying in a circle around me—but you
see, dear, I am an adult, and I know where to draw the line.
I have the maturity to say, this is only my imagination, and
I am not going to pay attention to it. Even though they
seem real enough to count: three, six, nine, twelve—there
are thirty birds circling Mama's head, making her dizzy. But
that's backwards. Mama is dizzy from not having sleep and
all the commotion, and so, Mama *imagines* the birds. Do you
understand the difference? It's very important. I think that's
the part of your education your Papa and I neglected. But
we'll fix all that now; it's not too late.

Anyway, as I was saying, when I read the silly article,
I thought, well, if any child could remember all that it would
be our Clara. So I wanted to ask you, dear, if you do remember? I mean, if you *think* you do—have a sense of how
it was for you in there, in Mama's tummy? I know it's ridiculous. But I wonder if you could feel my caring then, in
that perfect time. Once you told us you remembered a palm
tree, before you were born; and there was a palm tree outside
our hotel on our honeymoon in Bermuda—right outside our

window. Could you see Mama and Papa lying on the beach under that special palm tree—Papa putting the beach ball into Mama's tummy? You little tiny beach ball inflating in my tummy, then bouncing in me so big? Clara, I don't want you to think I am giving in to my imagination or that I'm setting a bad example, but just for a minute Mama is going to get your butterfly net again and pretend to catch just one of those imaginary birds because she's feeling a bit faint.

[She rises and walks unsteadily toward the net, stoops slowly to pick it up, and shakes the soot from it.]

Maybe you could try to feel it now, Clara: that being-in-my-tummy feeling? It might be a way of starting over for us. All of us.

[She returns to her chair only to set the net down again and resume her knitting. Each gesture is performed with great deliberateness.]

A way to go back in time, to when our love was . . . I can't think of the word, but I'm sure you could tell me, from all your studying . . . is it symbiotic? That time when our rhythms were perfectly aligned, just as they'd be now, if you'd only come sit with me, knitting, our hands moving in one motion, dancing with each other in a way. It would calm Mama if you would. Otherwise she might have to keep jumping up and doing things, getting distracted.

[Her eyes rest as often on the butterfly net as on the yarn in her lap. Finally she reaches for it.]

This will only take a minute, Clara. Maybe you'll appear after I take care of this nuisance.

[With the pole in her hand, she jumps up, trying to scoop one bird from the air into the net. After several unsuccessful attempts, she captures one, but only momentarily, because it breaks through the netting, with all the other birds in a chain behind it. They circle around and around *through the torn net, as if threading a needle. When the mother surrenders her grasp and releases the handle, the winged chain becomes a ring of fire.]*

Could you be my little parcel again, honey? Just for a minute? *[she pauses to catch her breath]* Pretend you're back there. Let's go away from all this confusion. Be my burdensome bundle of joy like some special possession that never gets put down, no matter how heavy, because it's so precious. Precious little baby Clara.

[The ring of fire now coalesces into a single gargantuan flame. Its texture—if flame can be said to have texture—softens. Its form seems malleable, for it squeezes itself through the hoop of the broken net and then expands again, explodes, ablaze with color: purple, red, azure, gold; color of fire and water both. Its huge body tapers to form a crowned head, and approximates the height of the ceiling.]

Clara, if you can see what I see now, I don't blame you for hiding. I'd like to hide myself, if I could find your special place. But we'll get this under control, too. Whatever this is, Mama will find a way to take care of it. Maybe it really came in through the chimney, just like Santa Claus, and it can go out the same way. They say bats can make themselves very tiny to get through the smallest openings. And this— whatever it is—seems to have that same ability to adapt itself. If you'd open that window like I asked you—well, I'll do it—then it might go out that way—or did you open it already? Let's open them all. It must be almost dawn by now; don't you think, dear?

[The mother creeps with her back against the wall, standing as far back as she can from the towering animate form, inching toward a window, opening it, proceeding toward the next, but never ceasing to speak.]

Do you know, Clara, I think you have something of that ability too. I think you could make yourself into a little compact ball, right now, so I could hug you tight. We'd be all warm and close then, nothing between us anymore.

[The girl's mother retires to the sofa, weary of her ordeal. She has had little sleep. Although far from relaxed, she dozes for a few minutes. And she dreams. She dreams that Clara is on a journey, and that she is safe. Her daughter, in the dream, is climbing upward, carrying her mother in her arms. As she wakes, she sees the creature of feather and fire radiating outward, igniting, as it were, into flight. As if a fan from outside were sucking it through the open window, the fire, rising, burns away the clouds. At last she recognizes the disc that seals together earth and sky in one grand healing gesture.]

The present and the past, which seem to us vast landscapes, as tangible as earth, have actually no integrity until resolved as trinity, in future. When we think of these packages of memory and experience as discrete entities, we lead ourselves into error. Clara knows this now. The perceptions to which she clung as life rafts were in truth no more substantial than the metaphorical body of water they might float upon. Isolate, such units are illusory, untenable; and the more tenaciously we cling, the more they slip.

To see instead the flow from past to present into what has yet to be is to be less deceived: to see there is continuum which cannot be, except artificially, arrested. Clara's mother cannot fully know this yet, but on this night she has drawn closer. She and Clara's father did not intend this lesson when they ostensibly denied their daughter validity of memory. But even inadvertent teaching must be given credit.

[The mother feels she has somehow waited all her life to witness this extraordinary sight, of night transformed into infinite light; even the miracle of birth seems ordinary in comparison. And yet the night has been so protracted, how could one not feel a sense of climax, closure? It is difficult to separate what she sees from what she has dreamt. But as she surveys the almost blinding rising sun, she hears distinctly song:

all the partial melodies of dawn becoming one hauntingly beautiful crystalline lyric, whose clarity and volume are such as to be audible to the ends of the earth.]

> The idea that bird-song is often an expression of ir-responsible joy or similar emotion is certainly not without some scientific justification and can, in fact, be supported by arguments which are far from neg-ligible. It may indeed be true that songs of birds can be regarded as the first step towards true artistic cre-ation and expression; and so it follows that birds were probably the evolutionary pioneers in the develop-ment of 'art', certainly preceding by immense stretches of time the development of artistic activities by the human stock.

Now there is no stopping the girl's creation, her perpetuation: secret to unceasing song. Her mother cannot quite see what or where her daughter is, and may never solve the mystery of what became of her. Perhaps she will, for some time, feel frustration, guilt or anger for what might be perceived as unavailability. Even annihilation.

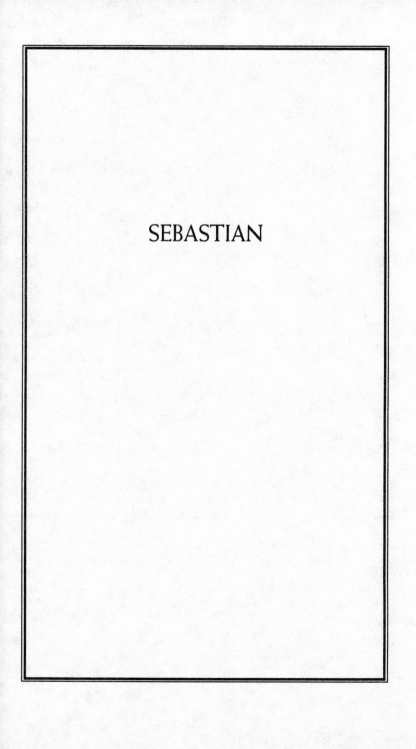

SEBASTIAN

BACK IN TEN READS A PIECE OF paper taped to the door of the small filling station, one of the few remaining non-self-serve, where Sebastian always goes because he likes the idea of service—that moribund concept—and as it happens, the only one whose logo matches that of his credit card. He's driving himself to the plane, leaving the car in the long-term lot, provided it's not full up—unlikely it would be. Then he'll drive himself home the next day, exhausted, because he and his—well, she is his fiancée, now, isn't she?—have a formalized agreement not to take advantage of each other in what she terms "gender specific" ways. His business advice on opening her own shop is somehow exempt from this category; taken for granted with perfect justification. In contrast, however, having packed his things: some clothes and toilet articles, for this sudden business trip, she decides she oughtn't rearrange her own appointments—having already made that ten minute contribution to his welfare—and lose sleep tomorrow night, or the next night or next, depending, to drive him now to, then from, the airport.

She'd shame him for indulging in a taxi: "All that distance, both ways," as well as gently, or not so gently, mock him for his excessive solicitousness toward his sports car, which he washes weekly, waxes monthly, lest any scratch or dirt mar the brilliance of its gleaming British Racing Green exterior. Sebastian suspects Sarah harbors secret affection for the outrageous vehicle but she'd surely not admit it. Clearly she does not fully appreciate it as she cannot even accurately pronounce its name, and turns his teacherly corrections against him when he revises the number of her syllables: not jagWAR, love: jag-u-ar. She'll say he exaggerates her error, and he'll say she his correction. But when he admits to fretting ever since he read in the local paper of an elderly woman who on her way out of the lot absentmindedly hurled her vehicle onto an innocent Trans Am parked in the same—escaping with merely a nose-bleed: the woman, Trans Am less fortunate—she wags her index finger patronizingly and tells him, "Seebee-Baby, what a jack-you-are."

"Very well, then," says Sebastian, "quite alright, I'll fetch myself. You needn't trouble." He even left early so as to be able to negotiate the possible though again unlikely traffic jams, and any such emergency hindrances in the lot, but he hadn't been, shall we say, psychologically prepared, to find the petrol station shut the very moment he pulls in. It's not that he hasn't the cash—how much would he need, after all? Granted, there are no other stations on this particular route, but it isn't that either; a matter of principle. Call it stubbornness. Sarah would: his tragic flaw, she'd say; one of. In any case, he's got ten minutes and he knows there's another errand before he goes; what was the thing he meant to write down, that he mustn't forget?

The dry cleaner's. His suit—that is, the trousers to his suit. He has the jacket but Sarah hadn't picked up the trousers to go with it. He can't figure that one; it's almost less—well, yes it is less convenient to have half a suit than none, and she insists she handed in the little yellow slip to get the jacket back and if the pants got lost somehow, she's not responsible. It's the cleaner's fault—if Sebastian is sure he gave the whole suit in the first place. He has been known to be absentminded about that sort of thing. Though obsessively meticulous about others?

He can already visualize the comic poster with ghoulish face, teeth bared, fist raised, and the cartoon dialogue bubble containing the words, "WHAT DO YOU MEAN YOU FORGOT YOUR SLIP?" He imagines Sarah might have penned the image. She did such drawings for shops and the like: miniature depictions of croissants or bean curd or children's clothes, to grace menus, posters, catalogues—the humbler early projects of her artistic career: pragmatic ones. Regardless of whose rapidograph that ink flowed from, he dreads the embarrassment, because he would never be at a loss for the receipt of a transaction: always there, neatly tucked away in his billfold, but now he must go like a penitent to the place and explain, about this cock-up caused by his premarital personal life.

No, the idea is unbearable; he will not, cannot. But this is obviously the opportune time to go to the dry cleaner's and solve the mystery. Oh, all he asks of life is to let him be invisible. And here he is, intimate with a woman whose appearance (striking features, indefectible body) and behavior (extreme, often indecorous conduct) attract no end of attention; although to be the companion of a beautiful woman does, in a way, achieve invisibility, as oneself is less noticed. And yet one is part of a unit which is constantly . . . on display.

Usually in private she'll allow him the spotlight, and make an appreciative audience indeed. For instance, she'll shout out, "Why, Sir Basil? Tell us why!" to Sebastian, whose imitation of Basil—not, to his knowledge, knighted—Rathbone, though he never saw or heard the man, is thoroughly convincing, as Sebastian proclaims, standing, from the center of the bed, with one arm pressed to his heart, the other stretched out before him, "We are the invisible immigrants." That is his cultural legacy, personal history, he explains to her: to be a member of this ostensibly preassimilated group, given so-called common language et cetera, to be one of the charming, witty and thus favored although by the same token entirely overlooked British in America. As few would consider them displaced, they might remain ever alien—might one say exacerbatedly alien, precisely because of that subtle if profound disparity between seem and be. They might even require, as a result, special attention. While Sebastian has nothing against—does in fact crave—certain kinds of attention, the more especial the better, he endeavors to explain to Sarah that in most instances, certainly most mundane, public instances, he relishes invisibility, strives to cultivate it, and might he implore her assistance rather than resistance?

"But Sebastian," she protests, "you should want to be noticed, to make your mark. And not be so embarrassed by things I do or say. Try to understand my heritage: a whole people almost annihilated. One man's organized movement to erase us from the earth!"

He's bothered by her use of the adjective "organized" in this context, for being that, i.e. having an orderly existence, is the closest thing Sebastian has to being invisible; and this lost piece of paper a perfect example of how she—inadvertently?—thwarts it. A trifling thing, granted: the slip. But isn't marriage, in part, an attempt to appreciate the largeness, for the other, of certain little things; to become, as it were, a student of just such subjective "little" things? He will make a point of explaining, again; not scold, but explain; how difficult can it be to convince someone of the patently obvious fact that the Holocaust has nothing whatsoever to do with a little yellow slip of paper? Travesty of the discursive. In any case, he does need those trousers for his meeting, the trip. At last he decides he will take a stroll over, and see then, if he can somehow summon the courage.

"BACK IN FIFTENE." What's this, an epidemic? says Sebastian, to himself—that is, out loud, but addressed to himself, annoyed—to the sign, to the door of the shop, to some inanimate ear. No, to the sign: hastily scrawled, misspelt, and naturally no indication of the time it was placed on the locked door. That's America, thinks Sebastian. That's America all over. If Napoleon disparagingly labeled England "a nation of shopkeepers," what then might one call this nation, which cannot even competently accomplish that function?

Now he really is cross with Sarah; he suspects she deliberately lost or neglected to fetch the trousers because she resented the task; it seemed too domestic to her. Or does she suspect the suddenness of his trip is indication of foul play? A secret liaison; last fling before the die is cast (or knot tied)—it, as it happens, isn't. She'd even make fun of the way he'd say it: *sewt*. But now it's his turn to feel resentful, a good bit, especially given that they are engaged to be married, the day looming. She was the one, after all, who insisted in the first place, those fifteen months ago, on doing things for him: the washing and so forth, the straightening, when truth be told she wasn't so able a straightener as he. She'd claim her disarray was creativity, expressiveness, and then she'd say, "Don't piss me off, Sebastian," when he went over again what she'd already done: the dishes, for instance. She could never make them squeak.

Fifteen minutes. And Sebastian has already waited five, he would wager. Of all the days to forget to wear his watch. His Rolex. Just that gesture of shooting the cuff to regard its face: familiar, consoling. He forgot, or subconsciously registered Sarah's perpetual derision. He cringes to think of the parties, at which she (a wee bit under the influence) might theatrically rattle off anecdotes, dated jokes, each in poorer taste than the previous: "How do you tell a rich Biafran (or was it Ethiopian?) from a poor? The rich one has the Rolex round his waist." Of course she told it more elaborately, the punch line long suspended. He can't recall the filler, or which party. But his crimson face, how warm it felt: indelible.

Worse still is what comes later. She'll chide him: "Funny piece of jewelry for a Marxist," alluding to certain theoretical interests he'd espoused during university. "Funny jewelry for jewelry, I'd say," he'll boomerang, referring to the artifacts she makes and sells; they're anything but delicate, or feminine in the traditional sense: hefty bracelets that wind toward the armpit (chastity bracelets, he jokes) or pendulous, threatening shapes that pierce the ear at seemingly more sites than a lobe could accommodate. Squared shapes that should be round; round that would be better squared. She says he can't appreciate her art.

"But do observe, my dear, the narrow space which falls between the *r* and *t* in the word you claim I've no appreciation for, and there insert that member of the alphabet which naturally would occur in this position (now elided) to substitute for *t;* complete the word with silent *e,* and we have remedied the problem of appreciation. Have we not?"

"Run that by me again, S.B.—only man whose jokes needs footnotes . . ."

"A hint, love. I might quarrel with the soldered shapes which bear your mark, but never could I praise sufficiently the shapeliness of their creatress."

"Oh, yes, I see." She's smiling now. "But could I have a compliment that's not a quiz some time?"

He's about to do it a dozen times (shoot his cuff), that businesslike, placating, right-angled twisting of arm, deft as a swimming stroke; and eventually catches himself before he must endure the sight of his ludicrous naked wrist. It feels somehow obscene, the unbound flesh. There's a clock in the car—or as Sarah says, "GWAR"; "take a ride in your GWAR"—but never any parking in these shops downtown, and always rather a hike from the meter to one's destination. He may as well have left the treasured vehicle blocking the pump at the filling station to make the irresponsible lad feel remorse when he returns from playing hookey: deserting his post, his pump. Come, now. Give up; it's not even a pun.

Given that this second expedition originated as a way to kill; let's say fill, time, while waiting for his trousers (the original thwarted transaction) this is very ill-advised: this additional, indefinite waiting. He thinks, without even meaning to evaluate, that just the combination of venting annoyance and reflecting on a course of action has taken ten. Ten what? Fifteen what, he often wants to ask of such signs as these. Declare the unit to which you refer. Soon it's twenty, certainly well past the time he could have promised himself to leave; but now, having waited this long already and with its being the second trial of the sort confronting him in a single morning, he feels compelled to wait still longer, with the rationale that it must be any moment now.

It reminds him of feeling equivocal about, for instance, a

certain phone call, that one needs to work up courage to execute—Sebastian is shy when it comes down to it—finally forcing oneself to ring, then ironically becoming, through the catalyst of that *beep beep beep*: torture sound that makes of respectable gentlemen nearly homicidal maniacs—becoming, out of defiance and in response to that stimulus of unavailability, of obstacle, quite determined to take the phoning through to conclusion.

The thing about Americans, Sebastian has always felt—and time has served only to reinforce this judgment—is that they don't take language seriously, violating the sanctity of morphemes: THANX and PIX and NU and &: ampersands respectable enough symbols until they deteriorate to apostrophe N. THIS N' THAT. Or WHILE-U-WAIT. Brutal distortions, abbreviations, degrading shorthand. Chaotic constructions: *winningest* of all? Now, that's obscene. Moreover, it's humiliating to be standing in front of this door, the victim of some spurious; no, simply fallacious message, that for some reason, or for the aforementioned reasons, he feels unable to dismiss. That is, at least, how he would defend his position, the closest thing he has to religion: to take language seriously, even if it gravely inconveniences him. It is, yes, a matter of principle. He feels he somehow owes it to language to wait, to miss the plane if need be, in order to see his mission all through. Absurd, granted, but that's how he feels right now. He'll wait. Nonchalantly, but he will wait, so he walks away from the door and the mocking sign, to the sidewalk, to the corner—there's a fair amount of traffic—where there isn't any stop sign but there should be.

What he wants, beyond access to the shop, of course, is not to appear to be waiting; not, at least, for this specific purpose. He wants to blend in, as one does in a foreign country; and as he, we know, almost always wants: not to appear conspicuous. Sebastian gets his wish. For after a while, it's clear he can't be waiting for any particular bus, as each has deposited and collected passengers twice or more. Yet clearly there is some relation to a man waiting for a bus. People begin to use him as a bus shelter. He can't provide interior capaciousness; nonetheless they lean against him. It consoles them, offers a sense of stability, permanence.

After a time, Sebastian feels he understands the rush and lull of life, thinks of individuals in service professions, how it must be to await, each day, the lunch or supper-time crowd, preceded and followed by uneasy solitude. Perhaps the tailor, in response to such a lull, allowed herself this ostensibly respectable hiatus. Although at first he'd felt unsettled by the contact, Sebastian comes to feel abandoned when whole parties board their bus and leave him stranded once again.

When the rain falls, he does prove inadequate. What's the use of stability when one's getting wet? Even so, people are reluctant to dismiss him. They take him for a rubbish bin, tossing toward his person straw wrappers and other crumpled paper; even a small glass bottle dropped into his waistcoat. But again he has limited capacity; he is principally surface, not depth. Before he can blink, they're using him as a bicycle rack, leaning their transport between his legs, securing the wheel to his arm. That's what happens, he thinks, when one has a free wrist. And after the rain stops, when they wish to be unencumbered, an umbrella stand. A passing pug dog lifts its leg and aims: "Oh that's really too much," Sebastian says, "what do you take me for? I'm more than some receptacle for waste or scorn or circumstance." But still he is an ashtray, a spittoon; there's something old-fashioned he exudes: a comfortable if obsolete civility that invites yet cannot be left unsoiled. Sebastian has never felt so versatile in all his life. Nor so defiled. He finds ashes in his breast pocket. Drool on his tie. I hope, he thinks, there might be a missing dress shirt with those trousers, so I can change this one.

It had occurred to Sebastian, in the midst of these abuses, that the tailor, the owner of the dry-cleaner's, might be on her lunch hour, though it seemed it couldn't be already noon. Yet now he is confused by the sight of uniformed children populating the sidewalk, as if school had let out for the day, and thus it would have to be an awfully protracted lunch hour the woman was taking. Though in either case, it would have been only common courtesy to make an honest declaration rather than the dangerously optimistic assumption that a quarter hour would prove sufficient. But of an individual who cannot even spell— and so many of them there are—what can one expect?

He should go back, back to the sign itself, if only because soon there will be children everywhere, and Sebastian knows children can also be abusive; his stamina is waning. He supposes it could be their lunch hour as well, for which they, living near, are permitted to go home, and this realization momentarily distracts Sebastian from his perturbation by causing him to reflect upon how different an experience school must be for a child when he or she can come home every afternoon (perhaps even twice in an afternoon) and return the following morning. In other words, one would associate returning with home rather than with school. This provokes, for no logical reason really, an image of his mother, many years ago, not in this particular instance—curiously enough—inebriated; buying him a gold-plated pen and pencil set, was it?—at the airport—the usual showering of gifts before separation, before his boarding to return to school, a small boy on a large plane. He recalls being at first too shy but then, somewhere over the Atlantic, finding the courage to show it to the stewardess, she making much of it.

Right after the divorce, he thinks it was: the time he hadn't been able to go home at all. Just the trip to see her and back to school. And his father came for the day shortly after, took him on an outing. Where had they gone? But this plane; what of it? Now that he is much older, and only asks the stewardess for a gin and tonic (one: genetics of alcoholism) and feels disappointed that the airlines seem to have rather more matronly stewardesses than once they did. Or perhaps he is more choosy. Or are they all aging together, he and they? In any case, even the fetching ones don't offer more than momentary arousal because arousal is now bound to Sarah in his psyche; her abundance his trap; he almost resents her for that: that she satisfies him so completely.

Though the fairly frequent business trips essentially bore him; the one, two or three nights away fill him with such anticipation that he cannot wait to return to her bed, his desire providing more than ample fuel for the journey and compensation for having to drive himself back, no one to embrace and welcome him when he steps off the plane. But she will wake for him, and be eager as he: this he can always depend on. It's his own fault when there's trouble, in those instances.

"My love is like a battery," he'd said one such time. "I know," she'd said, her arms stretched out to exaggerate receptivity: "Everready." She was so happy. And he had to ruin it, had to add, "The poet John Donne compared love to a compass." Then her "I know" was angry and hurt: "I know that, Sebastian. I've known it since high school. And you don't have to say 'the poet, John Donne,' like I'm some idiot and you're some professor. Why do you have to do that? What are you proving? This is a bedroom, not a classroom. Talk dirty to me instead; don't whisper that in my ear. I can't stand it!" And the accusations of pompousness and condescension—though they border on hysteria—are acknowledged, this time, as accurate. He was only grateful he had spoiled it in the middle of the night, after they'd already once reunited; had it been earlier he would have felt unbearably bereft.

Thinking of his forthcoming opportunity for atonement— he will do better; will please her, not be stupid—it's insecurity, that's what—not vex her—he finds himself looking forward, quite excitedly, to the trip (as departure is prerequisite for return) and its indirect rewards. Yet here even its initiation is impeded. He must move things toward expediency. He must extricate his sullied self from this precarious corner; it is simply too hazardous waiting unaccompanied, and as such exposed. He chose a mode too passive; in that was his error. He will now take action, return to confront the sign; he will force it to yield. A quarter hour, he thinks, might well have passed by now.

* * *

With his resolve to activate every mental gesture he has inadvertently uttered the statement aloud. An inquisitive grunt startles him. "I beg your pardon," Sebastian hastens to add, as if he'd sworn; "I was just thinking of my trousers." When he sees that the grunt would appear to have emanated from an overweight middle-aged woman, he feels compelled to say again, "I beg your pardon"—feels now he has the hiccoughs—and isn't sure himself whether the involuntary apology is meant to circumvent a misinterpretation of his words: they might, he fears, be misconstrued as metonym of male—or directed toward the original utterance: the breach of silence.

"Yeah, yeah, my dress," says the woman with a dismissive wave of her pudgy hand, followed by a turning of the palm toward herself, as if she were obliged to make these perfunctory introductions: "Dress, I would like to introduce trousers. Trousers, dress. How do you do?" The apology could easily have been spared, and the metonymy an accurate, yet not offensive interpretation. The woman, continuing to wave her hand now that she'd set it in motion, as if their mutual inconvenience were heat that could be fanned away—heavy people do feel the heat more, recalls Sebastian—soon grows bored of the gesture and lodges her body against the building, ceasing all motion to smile beatifically at Sebastian, as if all were resolved by the occasion of this coincidence: this bond.

Being thus scrutinized, though far from critically, reminds Sebastian, who prides himself on being well groomed, of his dishevelled appearance (which he can assume without a mirror's proof) and he feels uncomfortable. More so when he realizes there are others, each with the same objective as himself and his new "companion" and hence the same difficulty. The more eyes potentially upon him, the more nervous Sebastian feels; wishes he could slip away, shower, change, return, and then before he can protect himself—how would he protect himself?—an unsavory looking fellow approaches and begins, not to chat, but harangue, standing near and making the sort of eye contact that traps one: large brown eyes and silly hair that's short on top but made into a long skinny braid at the back. He begins his assault with deceptive nonchalance: "Gotta cigarette?"

Sebastian assumes he is not the first victim but feels none-theless singled out; thrown off by the recent unsettling incidents, he was easy prey, his guard down: vulnerable. "Sorry." He knows this will not be enough to brush him off.

"Hey, you live around here?"

"No . . . well, yes. Yes . . . and no." The brown eyes seem not to blink. Sebastian wishes he knew what strategy to take but he's only confused. Being standoffish seems to have no effect whatsoever.

"Know what?" Oh God, if only he could elude the nuisance.

"No. What?" Perhaps if he matches syllable for syllable, giv-ing only the minimum, as so many here speak anyway, the pest will become frustrated and try elsewhere.

"I'm running for president."

"Can't vote." For once Sebastian is happy for the circumstance of his foreignness and opportunity to report it.

"Huh?"

"Not a citizen, you know. Can't vote. Can't run."

"Can't run?" Sebastian wishes he could, right now, physically run away, is tempted to say—no, it would make things worse—so simply says, "for office." Compulsively he feels he must explain to the half-wit, so that he understands. He says each word slowly: "Because I am not a U.S. citizen, I can neither vote"—he pauses—"nor can I run for public office . . . such as you are . . . or claim, to be doing. Is that clear then?"

Sebastian thinks perhaps now he has the wherewithal to disengage this public nuisance. For some reason, whenever he is instructing about something, imparting information, he feels se-cure, strengthened, less threatened. Still something irks him about the fellow, and his new-found sense of control begins to erode when he realizes that even more than the man's offensive manner, it is an association, of Sarah's, shall we say, past life: many partners, undiscriminating. Every so often some unbidden thought will bring on the anxiety, manifest by a sensation resembling sudden contact with some slimy thing. Fleeting, yet resonant. Hard to shake off.

That bloke in New York, for instance, with the earring, whom they'd run into on the street when Sebastian accompanied her to the jewelry show. Embraced right there in the street. "An old friend," she'd said. Another, he'd thought. He knows what those earrings mean on men. And when he tried to voice his worry, she declared, "I won't restrict my life out of fear. How could I anyway, in retrospect? Besides, you're an elitist; you judge so much by appearances."

Though that night, in all fairness, she did attempt to reassure him: "It's just you, you know, from now on. Always. We're engaged, aren't we? Sebastian? Aren't we, my Starburst?"

Curious that she could make such a reversal. He can't help questioning it, but makes little headway when he tries to question her: "Isn't it funny, Sarah, someone unconventional as yourself, desiring something so conventional as matrimony?"

"No funnier than someone conservative as you, having such resistance to the proposal. No funnier, for that matter, than the two of us together in the first place."

It often seems to him he cannot win, for when he is the enthusiast, she suspects ulterior motives, namely his quest for citizenship; then next day she'll flip the coin and amplify his minor doubts. Of one thing he is certain: the need to shed the unwelcome company imposed on him now, and he announces his departure to all present.

"I beg your pardon." Why can he come up with no better a formulation? Is the fat woman smirking? "I am now setting off to find the tailor, if you please, and will return as soon as that is accomplished." Sebastian feels a charlatan but justified under the circumstances. The presidential candidate seems impressed. It's not as if he is departing under false pretenses, after all; he will seek the tailor. It is certainly in his own as well as everyone else's interest to do so.

He does not gaze back as he walks. Why had he left these tasks for today? Two seemingly simple errands. If only he'd done them yesterday, instead of what—well, who's to say what might have gone wrong with something else? Perhaps anything he'd attempted would have been obstructed. All arbitrary. Is it his fate? His karma, as Sarah would say. For it seems to Sebastian that if he chooses what appears to be the shortest queue of cars proceeding toward a toll, inevitably by the time he reaches the unmanned booth that blocks his way, the tire of the car ahead will suddenly deflate; or in the anomalous instance of an actual person guarding the toll, the previous driver will require detailed explanation of directions. Or worse still, the same individual behind the wheel will choose that moment to demonstrate his clumsiness and thus be required to exit the vehicle so as to grope on hands and knees—needless to say awkwardly—for the small round glimmer that should not, for all the world's logic—or is it physics—have been able to stray any farther than directly under the electronically feeling basket.

The same applies to checkout at the market, even the so-called express lane. When he and Sarah shop together it is different; he is distracted: she shows him the fashion magazine models as she pages through, asks his opinions, makes suggestive facial expressions, despite what she knows to be his embarrassment at being seen regarding such reading material. It isn't necessarily a less stressful procedure with her company (given their agreement they alternate the responsibility and on weekends combine forces) but he finds himself less squeamish to watch the cashier's clumsy utilization of the ocular scanning device, as she smears whatever item, brutally, several times, to make it "read." He does not care at all for the black and white bars that resemble some distorted miniature keyboard, reducing every item on earth to number, whose identity can be registered in an instant.

She'd say there's nothing special in his feeling that; she'd say it only means he is a human being. Still, the contours of his feeling aren't generic, he'd insist. No, on the contrary, highly nuanced. More than she could ever know. Or does she know? In either case, she's sure to be annoyed at his annoyance when they find themselves, on that very express lane, behind a woman who decides that in honor of the frugality of purchasing ten or fewer items, she will pay the cashier all in pennies. "An admirable woman such as this," he'll whisper in her unreceptive ear, "would never take a taxi to the airport. Am I right, love?" She'll merely roll her eyes and reach behind the next impatient customer to show him *Vogue* or *Elle*: some even more salacious pose that he would gladly linger over in their boudoir but which here in the Star Market only makes the blood rush to his face and ears, that same warmth he feels more often than he'd like; recalls the time, after being similarly annoyed at the toll booth, he became so flustered that he neglected to make the simple pressure of finger that would electronically roll down the Jaguar's window and flung his coins against the glass. To spare himself the memory's intensity, he finds himself imagining this woman with her pennies making weekly, even daily pilgrimages to toll booths so as to scour for the products of such mishaps as that endured by the aforementioned—if hypothetical—clumsy man, who to his credit did at least manage to get his change outside the car.

At this moment, however, Sebastian is liberated from any queues; he is mobile, observing others in them. He realizes the liberation is deceptive, and after only moments finds himself melancholy, envious of the luxury enjoyed by others accomplishing their tasks. The yearning he has rarely felt in his life, as for some object—the yearning most people know all too well, as they peer through the glass of some shop window to covet a prohibitively expensive item (Sebastian usually knows how to obtain what he wants materially)—is here approximated in a strong desire to trade places, as Sarah would say, with almost any of the customers he views going through the motion of these poignantly ordinary activities.

She sometimes says, "I'd like to be that girl for a day: have her body, her thoughts, her habits. Or you, Sebastian, for an hour, to understand you better. Or just for a minute, one of those women who can't come."

"Really, Sarah, you are patently absurd at times."

"But I wonder how it feels."

"Probably quite frustrating."

"What, to be you? Or them?"

"Both, love."

"Have you ever been with a woman who can't?"

He might have replied, "Yes, but they are soon transformed," and that would have pleased her: that confidence, rather than being threatened by the intimacy of such a question. She would have winked and said, "Oh yes, I do understand."

This time, fortunately, she is not offended, not scolding; instead turns it into a game, insists they pretend to be strangers, the bed a berth on a ship or train, and he must blindfold her, or they each other. An enormous expenditure of energy is his lover, but unfailingly engaging. Charming is perhaps not quite the word.

Continuing to walk, Sebastian watches, from the pavement, the progress of the post office queue. He sees those who enter bearing heavy parcels and stacks of envelopes, retrace their steps in reverse, freed arms dangling, even swinging. The intimacy they have with their purchases, he thinks longingly, as he watches them put their tongues delicately to the gummed reverse side of shells, faces, flags; then repeat the ritual of tongue to gummed surface in order to seal the rectangular sheath that bears these smaller images.

Everything's coming up rectangles for Sebastian; he begins to see all in geometry, as he stands now before yet another queue, formed for the purpose of a single gesture: feeding a plastic rectangle into a slot. Soon after, he witnesses the cleanest regurgitation, accompanied by a sort of propagation, as each individual's index finger presses a pattern of four (which he imagines as the coordinates of other geometric figures) until emerge crisp paper rectangles almost impossible to peel away, one from another. He can guess that when those doing this errand go to spend what they have extracted, a particular shopkeeper might call them back to display great integrity when he reveals the ostensibly single bill as a twin.

Although Sebastian originally took on this search as a means of avoiding small talk, and disturbing thoughts, he is now like a man obsessed with locating a lost lover or elusive criminal. He is intent on finding her in some queue, and yet he barely recalls the tailor's description. He had a fitting once, did he not?—Seems long ago, for often it's Sarah who brings the clothes; she's the clothing person, after all; another of her art forms. Perhaps she is this very moment cutting, or creating, a pattern for her wedding dress, undoubtedly like no bridal gown before or since. She threatens she may dye it green. "Whatever for, love? You wish perhaps to please my Irish grandmother? The one who wished on me this cursed Catholic name?"

"No, my dearest S o' B, just to be honest. It's the green card you're marrying me for, isn't it? The security of it: a quick way to a work permit before this other thing expires?"

Any reference to that I-151 form, the "alien" registration, gives Sebastian a queasy feeling, not unlike thoughts of Sarah's past, for it conjures images of slimy Mexican wetbacks, are they called? The card is all that separates them from himself. The card is ignominy enough.

"It is most certainly not why, Sarah. It is a small fringe benefit, you might say, analogous to the opportunity to change one's name, for a woman to change her name, when she marries. If you, for example, wanted to substitute my surname for yours . . ."

"I have no desire to do that. I like Zeidman just fine. I think you think it's proper for a woman to take her husband's name, and I think you don't like my name, and I think I know why you don't."

"It was only an example, to illustrate . . ."

"Since when are you the expert on illustration?"

It is impossible to predict what will set her off; sometimes it seems arbitrary, like a multiple-guess exam where you're more likely to be wrong than right. Oh the stupid, not even green— old ones with wavy green lines all across, new ones beige— rectangle; to be unburdened of the paradoxically weightless albatross, bad enough all on its own, now all the more problematic because Sarah makes it an issue. He can hear her playfully mimicking his drawn-out sibilance, followed by "you," instead of American *sh* as in *hush* plus the round sound she says when he makes her feel the way she likes best to feel. He can scarcely believe he has the power; her face transformed in passion, regarding his: amazed, flattered, reciprocally aroused, seems as much component of his pleasure as his pleasure. And no one else could ever grasp as skillfully, gingerly, completely without awkwardness his one retracting testicle: the stubborn one, she's christened it—"synechdoche for me, you mean? Is that it, love?"—persuading it to join its twin, participate.

"Do you know, Sarah," he confides, "after all those years of sedulous study, the pages of my biology book frayed, when my schoolmates with no women about had resorted to researching each other, I was consuming every possible detail of female anatomy, exterior and interior, imagining how to apply the knowledge toward pleasure, a woman's pleasure. Like medical students who yearn after years of memorization of factual information to get their hands on actual living bodies, I thought, someday I will put this to use, to good use. I want this: flesh, as my field of expertise."

"You have, darling, you truly have, and it is," she says, caressing him. "You get a gold star."

"High marks, do you mean? And how will you reward me?"

"In kind," she says, "as you would say. I'll reward you in kind." And she makes him close his eyes, whispers, "Now make a wish," proceeds to make herself completely his, in the guise of a game in which she must guess—she gets three—but not resort to verbal means. Only when this is accomplished can either speak, at which point she asks, "Would you like to find the sweetest path to sleep?" And even Sebastian surrenders the verbal in his response. When he wakes, she is gone, but in her stead a large elaborate mobile: hundreds of those sticky-backed gold stars on strips of colored paper and string, all cascading down, caressing him—how did she install it without waking him?—the morning sun making it even more radiant; feels like waking to a dream, and he thinks it's the most beautiful thing he's ever seen.

But when she's angry she'll taunt him: Sebastard. Or simply S.B. as implied reversal of the paired letters which stand as universal initials for what is not so, and should not be claimed. Is it more than coincidence, he wonders, that the animal whose excrement she obliquely alludes to is male? And when he is, as he's prone to be, excessively stubborn, she'll lop off the first syllable; Bastion.

"Sarah, do you fancy my name at all? My given name, I mean? You might try using it from time to time." Why, he often thinks—though fond of his name—couldn't I have been a Mark or a John, perhaps Ian: something distinct but too short to muck about with? Because that's the other thing about Americans: anything more than monosyllabic is subject to ridicule if not incomprehension.

In one of Sarah's costly art books is a reproduction of the saint he is namesake to, bearing the arrows. They gaze at it together, he occasionally allowing her to be the one imparting information. It is, after all, her field. Yet often her remarks are mere impressions: "The arrows are just garnish in most," she says. A curious perception.

"Do you prefer this, then, where the arrow's right through the head?—who's it by, Mantegna?—thank you very much. You do know he wasn't mortally wounded by the arrows?"

"Yes, I do know. Beaten to death, right? Glutton for punishment, like all those saints."

"Indeed. And as they are interchangeable in that respect, might we examine some other victim, just for variety? Saint Anthony, for example: the Sasetta painting we both admire. Assaulted by monkeys, you'll recall."

"Not so fast now, S.B. You can't run from who you are. Grandma Bowen might have had good intuition after all. I mean, think about it, a man who was doubly stubborn: first, to keep his religion a secret—something very important to him, a part of him, hidden; then, to go imposing it on other people, trying to make them be like him. It's no wonder . . ."

"Sarah, you are ascribing a great deal of significance to what is merely . . . onomastic coincidence."

"Now there's a nice word. Doesn't it have to do with men masturbating? Or dreams? Sebastian, did I ever show you the painting where he's holding his own arrow in his hands?"

"Could we change the subject?"

"But isn't torture like sex for saints?"

"I am not the expert, Sarah. Although narcissism acquaints me with the legend, I prefer to forget what I knew of hagiography. For God's sake, I'm not a bloody Catholic."

"I think you're avoiding something that you'll have to face sooner or later, Bastion. Even your friend John Donne—wasn't he the one who said coming was dying?"

Her imposed equations distress Sebastian, increasingly, although it does seem appropriate that the man appearing in image after image be thus afflicted. In point of fact, the many versions of the martyr throughout the history of art trouble Sebastian hardly at all; it is rather the proliferation of images of Sarah's inspired by the motif that give him pause. Her productivity around this theme is especially rich, in every medium. And Sebastian suspects he's seen only a fraction of her output. He is, by what through permission or stealth he has viewed, alternately flattered, threatened, often perplexed and simply befuddled. Dare he say he feels exploited, as women can claim at the drop of a pin, or pun; a hat or hoot?

Whatever to name the negative feeling, there is, to offset it, the ecstasy that only she can bring him, when her sweetness has no edge, when the barely audible names do not belittle but praise. Nor is he unaware that what appears to be gratuitous abuse has behind it some grander scheme, some greater goal: a vision for his "human development." This realization, a recent one, does not preclude resistance:

"Wouldn't it be easier, Sarah, to join the Peace Corps, if it's a mission you want? Go teach the natives papier mâché—something they can use?" He makes jokes about her procrustean efforts: calls the bed "iron" and her "giant," which makes them both laugh, as she, not much above five feet, has not the appropriate stature to bear his accusation.

Truthfully, now, does he try to shape her—often outlandish—conduct, beyond innocent lessons in linguistic, or grammatical improvement which fall on deaf ears? For some reason, it's being together in public that's worst: those parties. If she hasn't humiliated him publicly already, he knows there's something in store, such as the night he found himself cynosure and rather liked it, only to have the bubble burst when she assaulted him:

"Everybody finds Sebum charming."

"With one notable exception, at the least." He tried to make the banter real, to ask a probing question: "Why can't you, Sarah? Of all people, why couldn't you, just once, find me so?"

"Because I see through you." Her large light green eyes into his smaller blue sometimes seem to do just that, discomfit him.

"Then why"—he almost fears the answer—"do you stay with me? If the bottom of the pellucid pool is so much slime?"

"Guess I haven't Analyzed it," she quips, triumphantly lengthening the *a* to make further comment on his psychic constitution.

Case closed, he would suppose, though he's tempted to say, "Who's obnoxious, Sarah?" But when she's in that mood, that—admitted, slightly "altered"—state, one had best leave ill enough alone.

Now, having reached a laundrette, Sebastian watches the laden customers enter with plastic baskets and canvas bags overflowing with cloth. When he sees others like them emerge unburdened, he feels anything but analytical. He is jealous, yearns for their lightness, exaggerates in his mind the before and after: weight on earth vs. weightlessness in space. He sees himself walking in space, his feet gliding over the moon's surface. Then thinking of the coins (not rectangular, round) they feed into machines, he remembers the meter, that is, as it were, undernourished, severely. He wants not even a ticket to mar the beauty—and always the terror of towing. Unlikely they'd tow. Not in a marked zone. At the same time, he realizes that if he were now to go back to the car, he might very well miss the return of the tailor; he may have missed her already, although he has been desperately vigilant, remaining on the pavement, never actually entering any given structure. Still, she may have eluded him, for in spite of himself, he has been preoccupied.

He wouldn't mind some lunch himself. It must have been a midday meal toward which those schoolchildren were heading, he decides as he watches customers exit a delicatessen with wrapped sandwiches, coffee in styrofoam cups (nasty substance) which stand in partitioned cardboard boxes. Lunches for office mates, orders "to go." How long does each transaction take? Not long. Not at all long. Why could it not have been so with the seamstress? What might have detained her when it is possible to be expedient? Perhaps, jubilant at the efficiency of acquiring just such a sandwich, she became greedy, and undertook other less urgent but far more time-consuming expeditions. At least he could get himself some coffee. Tea's not real tea here. But without food, the caffeine might upset his stomach, when already he's queasy. More importantly, any, even such a small, diversion, might put his mission in jeopardy.

Stoical, Sebastian continues to walk. Sweet smells greet his nostrils, and their source becomes apparent when he sees, like soft stones, long loaves of bread; white boxes tied with blue and white twine, white waxy bags from whose ridged edges blossom every imaginable confection. One hand reaches into a bag the other hand holds and releases a tart with raspberries set into custard. Another hand finds a cookie, iced half black, half white, from which the affiliated mouth takes one bite black, then one bite white, and carries on the symmetrical consumption. She loves me, she loves me not, Sebastian thinks. That's how it feels. One day black, one day white. Back and forth.

Finally, as if for his private viewing, he beholds the pièce de resistance: a many-tiered cake—too tall to wrap, he supposes—with a plastic memento atop: man and woman of indefinite features, dressed in some silly approximation of nuptial costume, distinct as to gender only due to one's being painted black, the other white, rather than any mimic of physiological design, only slightly less amorphous than the chocolate/vanilla biscuit. Cookie. The buttery, sugary, lemony scents that graced his nostrils now begin to make Sebastian slightly nauseated. The word she'd use is nauseous, and if he corrected her usage she would playfully mimic his precise enunciation of separate syllables, undaunted by his accusation that she ridicules to distract, as she cannot bear to admit she's in error.

"Oh let me play, Sebastian, pretty please?" And even though she won't assimilate the correction, he cannot disapprove of the game that turns more and more to his advantage: "Izzy itsy Seebee naus-e-us? Naughty us will fix his naus-ee-us. Izzy getting sleepy? We know how to let him get some sleep." And one hand travels while the other takes his reticent appendage and gently calls it forth, emptying her mouth of syllables and finding substitutes. How Sebastian loves sex with Sarah, as if someone offered him the quintessential recipe for what was already his favorite meal.

And how he wishes he could, at this moment, partake; communion with that flesh as sacred, to Sebastian, as once felt thin round bread upon his tongue: such purity he felt within himself those once weekly mornings, during the years of fervor preceding equally ardent apostasy. He chose of his own volition, at no one's suggestion, to be confirmed, well past puberty, only to renounce before the age of twenty-one. He felt it might assuage his doubts to make that pledge, then regularly take bread, repeat the words that meant to make a miracle. A great many doubts Sebastian had: what others took for granted. Special sessions with the chaplain were so frequent during one period that the other boys said, "What did the padre preach you this time, Sebastian?" But he, somewhat ashamed and preferring privacy, never disclosed the questions that prompted such answers as, "The earth, Sebastian ..."—he remembers the use of his first name: intimate, gentle—"The earth will not likely cease to turn. We assume—and we must—that when we wake and move to place our feet upon the floor, that floor will be there to receive them." It should be a comic image in his mind: the earnest chaplain bending toward the frowning lad, grave beyond his years, but it isn't yet; poignant instead.

Once he tried to explain these things to some sort of analyst, here—it is so common here. He went for only a few sessions, and the certified individual: intelligent enough, fairly perceptive, he supposed, determined that, rather suggested that it was not unreasonable that Sebastian find reassurance in something so very nebulous as religion and its myths about transforming ordinary substances, as well as in something both so ordinary and extraordinary as the female body, given that his own relation to actual food and nutrition was quite precarious in his younger years. Sebastian had told of more than occasional instances of undernourishment alternating, unpredictably, with feasting, depending on his mother's "condition." He regretted, in a way, also to have revealed the little song his father would sing—hard to remember whose composition it was; collaboration most likely between father and son—to cheer themselves and distract from the prospect or fact of empty stomachs. The tune will always be with him: "Shepherd's Pie when Mum is dry; Spam when she's besotted." He smiles even now to think of it; that to him is funny, albeit poignant as well, though the "shrink"—that Americanism catching for one quite aptly the reductionist nature of the analyst—found no occasion to smile, saw only the tragic aspect.

It was mere game to himself at that time. He knew there was something naughty in it which made it all the more alluring; but a comfort too: just the sound of his dad's voice, a deep yet sweet, lyrical voice. Especially delightful when they abandoned all propriety, accompanying themselves with knives and forks against the table during the rousing repeated chorus and its minute variations: ". . . Spam when she's been sloshing"—except the time when she found them at it and such a row there was: a kind of coitus interruptus when they suddenly had to cease at the height of their performance. But that scene he has managed to block out, despite an attempt by the analyst, in the third and final session, to resurrect the details.

Sarah loves the ditty; she's the only other he's told. She appreciates it. He had little use for the analyst's conclusion except to make it into play—what she loves best—to make her laugh and eventually emit other sounds of pleasure, when he professed and manifested deprivation: "As I don't take the host any longer, Sarah, it's only you to nourish me and I require, I warn you, a great abundance to offset that early lack." He would pretend every inch of her was to be in some fashion consumed by him, and prod her flesh with tongue and teeth, while her mouth repeatedly rounded to exude the luxuriant sound he so loved to hear, until in her surfeit she begged for mercy. Even then unrelenting, he called her another kind of host, and he her parasite—"Don't be disgusting, Cebestial; you'll turn me off."—said he was henceforth attached for life, and must find new sites to burrow in when others are exhausted; and though she limply insisted there was no pleasure left in her, as he had fulfilled it all, he assured her he knew better than she, and proved himself by leading her, incredulous, yet again to her pinnacle.

For that confidence, she would never criticize. There, in eros and in language, he is most at home; feels himself home. That is why, he supposes—in addition to the obvious reason that when life is most unpleasant and discouraging, one dreams of the other extreme—he would at this moment like to review his favorite experience: the most healing, reassuring, nurturing, defining, in short, essential, of experiences. To remind him . . . of himself, of who he is. Looking for what or who is lost can put one's own identity in jeopardy—in a certain, not quite explicable sense.

So it seems to Sebastian, who feels himself becoming overwhelmed. He had learned to recognize, if not remedy, that sensation: like being carried away in the grip of some massive, frothing breaker, or being dragged down by the undertow. What good, then, to be a human, erect, when it is impossible to maintain that stance against the elements, whether they be natural, physical elements, or more abstract forces, which press against one? Consequently one cultivates resistance, which is not a pressing back, not a counter-force, rather a tensing, a shrinking, really—unlike the earth, which once cooled down, spins faster. All the lads remembered the lovely image, to illustrate the point—a kind of oasis of fantasy in his sixty-minute geology class—of the skater, her arm curved in toward her body to go round even faster, their imaginations not instructed to include the image of her tiny twirling skirt, revealing a cloth even closer to skin, that, though meant to be seen, seemed illicit.

Better, perhaps, to be a creature of instinct. He sees his precious silver beast, his more-than-mascot who rides atop the hood, beautifully crafted, small yet an emblem of energy. This paradoxical projectile remains horizontal, stationary, even as she sears the air with speed and grace, and guides Sebastian through dark or light, into the unknown, the infinite—makes him think of Sarah in her silly but not unbecoming artificial fur jacket, and the spotted cloth bag from the same thrift shop, both intended, with reddish-brown spots on beige background, to resemble a leopard or jaguar's pelt. The jacket sets off her hair fetchingly—though a bit tattered, who knows how many other hands have handled it?—and rhymes, for him, with her own fearless forging ahead against any obstacle, toward any arbitrary goal. She has shown him the series of Muybridge photographs in which the animal is slowly rotating its mass, but they do not capture that aspect of flight, of wildness. He prefers the leaping cat in the same book; for a man can stand and turn, but to leap without hesitation . . .

Seems it should have something to do with gravity, but he's ignorant; caught up as he was at university with humanities: literature, philosophy; had he only read physics at Oxford—though he couldn't have placed—he might understand more of the world, have a hope of achieving synthesis. All he understands is words, what can be gleaned from a dictionary's definition: "the force of gravitation, being, for any two sufficiently massive bodies, directly proportionate to the product of their masses and inversely proportionate to the square of the distance between . . ." It's that which grounds one, yes? Affixes one to where one ought to be? And which attracts, as in the pull of things toward or away. Like water: fluid on a ball, pulled down by earth, pulled at by the moon; and what's more, rolling fluid on a turning ball. Whereas a human body, such as his own, likewise pulled by earth's gravity, standing in water, might well be assaulted by towering, foaming ridges. The body could leap to emerge triumphant on the other side (at least until the next foaming ridge) or the body could turn itself, through its own force, into projectile, and risk riding all the way to shore, gasping, bedraggled; yet even a waveless body of water spells fear: fear which arises from knowing one's own body is of sufficient mass to sink to the bottom. Drown.

The moon, on the other hand, does not spin; shows only one surface, if several countenances. Its motion, its rhythm, is how we perceive the concealing, revealing, what portion in shadow. Phases, cycles, rotations; our bodies mostly water, while the moon tugs at the mysterious parts of women, pulling gently, 'til they bleed. She calls him tribal because he likes to lick—once took his white silk ascot, placed it between her legs, and who would ever guess what marked the other side of what went round his neck, his chest, beneath his ever-so-respectable waistcoat? To have always with him an element of what makes her woman; a talisman of their two earth-bound bodies which when together are released from gravity: weightless, as if in water or space. Their non-celestial bodies. "Sarah, is this the animal or divine in us?" Magic, she says, that in this life, two bodies could so perfectly . . . Of course, she claims that bodies keep going round: karma; a far less cogent theory than that which claims the earth was released from the sun, sent spinning, no friction to keep it from turning. It must be less cogent, mustn't it? Perhaps better to stick to the dictionary: ". . . especially the central gravitational force exerted by a celestial body such as the earth . . ."

"Sebastian, lad; think now. Isn't it true, that if you place one foot in front of the other, like so, the natural gesture of walking occurs?" The small boy nods his head forward, respectfully, several times. "You do not think to yourself, moment to moment, 'Can I truly rely upon these feet, these legs, to do the job that God intended?' " The boy nods his head slowly from side to side, but when he rises, he will dwell upon the sensation, of lifting leg, moving foot forward; it will seem, suddenly, not quite natural. "And so, dear lad, likewise the earth . . ."

She does not, he thinks she does not fear death; dread that transition. She says he's resistant to mystery. But what, he wants to ask, is the appeal of a closed door? For him is the terrible dread that in the space between—that void—he might lose memory of earth, of life, yet not possess the sight to see what lies beyond, if something does. "Sarah, keep your karma, and my vestigial saints as well. This"—as she hugs him inside, their fluids exchange—"is the after built into my life."

He dare not tell her Aristotle keeps him grounded—well, his own distortion of the *Physics*: archaic philosophical musings from a pretechnological age that it must seem even at face value. But certain passages, granted, out of context, hold such power for him. Book IV, for instance, chapter 4, a sentence he cherishes: "If then a body has another body outside it and containing it, it is in place, and if not, not." He's not sure why he tells her some things; others not. She'd not mind his distortion, as it's tribute to her. Why then, can't he share the single sentence? Fears she'll ridicule the source; his Western bias? Or force him to acknowledge even Aristotle can't provide a total terra firma?

What then is definite? Is there an infinite? Or merely some indifferent primal cause who sent the world spinning, then waved it goodbye?—like opening a shop, then abandoning—relying on momentum to sustain its rotation. She loves me, loves me not. Like setting someone's head spinning so he can't stop, but if some external friction causes him to, he'll feel dizzy in an unpleasant fashion, that in no way resembles the euphoria of the first phase; rather, nauseating, disorienting.

Now Padre, were the earth still, I'd never think to ask, "Will it begin to spin?" Stasis less precarious, while motion, it seems, must inevitably sometimes cease, even if only transformed to another kind, of motion. Things can be severed, interrupted, done away with; can they not? Bodies that breathe one day cease to be, all their elaborate motion of fluid and blood disrupted; the processing, healing, exchanging no more. Some piece from inside, for example, might break off—just as earth from sun—and block an essential passageway, or some normal cell distort itself. So who is to say what potential friction might one day accost the earth: some unbidden celestial body or particle in irregular orbit?

When he is overwhelmed, such as at present, he knows the only possible help is to break down into components the amorphous mass oppressing; to assure himself it can in fact be broken down, then plan strategy; whether to jump into the center and hope to emerge triumphant, or to allow himself to be pushed, horizontal, with tremendous force, all the way to land. "Lighten up" is the expression she uses, not without compassion, as one when about to sink might lighten the mass of one's body by taking a deep breath, thus altering gravity. But that is precisely the trouble: he's no idea in these instances, which is appropriate: to try to make himself heavier, so as to make a more substantial adversary against the elements; or, as she suggests, to become lighter, so as to . . . what? Diffuse oneself into whatever is pulling at one—because a less dense body, i.e. one with less mass than the mass of that in which it is immersed, will not sink, not drown, somehow float atop? But how to achieve? "Just ride the wave," she'd tell him. "Go with it. You're afraid to give up control." His worst fear is that thought, thinking, upon which he relies to create order, might be the very thing which leads him into chaos. Not thought in general, mind you: *his* thought, his brain, whose thoughts, like cells which distort with no warning. . . . Perhaps she is right; for if he were to give up the yearning for order— how could he, though?—at least there would not be that potential for thought to turn on him, against him.

Yet here there is none to surrender; he, things, are out of control. That is an objective assessment, though she might offer a contradictory, subjective one. Is it not logical, even noble, to attempt to gain control of a chaotic, incomprehensible situation? There is no question in his mind that he is victim: of Sarah's forgetfulness, or worse; of the tailor's irresponsibility; perhaps of something greater still. What could he have done to prevent this state of affairs? He supposes he might have rung before embarking on the . . . expedition. Fiasco. But in truth he cares not for the instrument, allegedly of convenience—of torture: his private pun—that Mr. A.G. Bell bestowed upon the world.

Now words are one thing; he's good with words, but when one takes away the person and leaves these oddly disincarnate sonic shells; well, what then? One has no more, no less than void: void masked as human contact. It's all Sebastian can sometimes do to lift the appropriate part of the insistent ringing apparatus and say to the anonymous annoyer, "Good afternoon, Sebastian speaking." Worse, of course, is the need to lift the thing and initiate communication, which is far more complicated than that other nearly passive gesture, somewhat like scratching an itch: needing, merely for the sake of peace to arrest the incorrigible ring. But the former, as it constitutes an ostensibly voluntary action, imposes upon the receiving party the necessity of executing the granted, less offensive but nonetheless unpleasant "defensive" action; that is, if one is fortunate enough to reach the other party, to achieve communication, for it is at least as likely, that after all the bother of preparing oneself to engage in this so-called communication, one be greeted with the horrid rhythmic rude noise that symbolizes temporary unavailability.

One becomes cross; tries to guess who, at that particular moment, is making life difficult, perhaps even ringing other numbers to ascertain possible villains, but of course it is misplaced blame. Why should the individual being summoned be held accountable for unavailability at any particular time? It is something mechanical that makes a wedge between the personal: a wedge in human communication. Anger mounts toward the party whom you wanted first casually, then desperately, to contact, and you feel slighted by the incidental circumstance of his or her being engaged with another. Or perhaps he or she has closed off all communication with the receiver uncradled. Even so, this is not something personal, yet it is taken as such. No, it is all of it impersonal.

Which is in fact the thing about America, where the term is to call—to ring seems more accurate, more "honest": to reduce to mechanics that gesture which no longer bears relation to "call upon," visit, have actual contact. Yes, call: properly an act made with a voice, to a friend or relation or lover; one calls: "Do come home now" to children at play; "Would you care to come by?" to a friend, to someone standing no farther than down the street: that is a call, but in this context blithely used as if this strange vehicle of transmission did not radically alter the act of saying, did not effect an entirely different breed of communication.

Things masquerading as what they are not evokes Sebastian's ire, such as this—far from forgotten—mendacious sign, scribbled by a woman, who, if Sebastian had thought to "call," would, if she'd answered, more than likely not have thought to mention this imminent foray into oblivion. Where could she be? Has she no sense of the contract embedded in language: the contract it, ideally, is? Those words, her scribbled words, he feels, should bring her back, from whatever irresponsibility or inconvenience or misfortune might be occurring, just as leaving something on the hob or in the cooker—word that never fails to elicit giggles from Sarah, as the latter is her own colloquialism for the unit in which she disinfects her small hydrophillic polymacon spheres that for most individuals substitute for spectacles, but in her case, are merely vanity's playthings, when she fancies a change—on a low heat of course, will, he feels, prevent him from having an accident. It's something about responsibility to others: the anxiety (paradoxically protective) that arises from knowing that flame sits under that vessel, this very anxiety will bring him home unharmed by fate to ensure that others' fates are left neutral. Not quite rational, he realizes.

It's a way of challenging fate, he supposes—"the earth will not likely cease to turn"—of claiming confidence, demanding from life a guarantee: nothing, in the next twenty-four hours, will happen to me. Things will proceed as planned, without impediment, and I have a curious, not quite tangible talisman to prove that. He nearly divulged this to the certified individual in the third session when he was asked, "Is there anything else associated, even tangentially, with food?" but the words wouldn't exit his mouth, and he'd already decided there'd be no next session. Sebastian has heard of an exercise, designed by similarly certified individuals working with perhaps certifiable individuals, where one must fall, deliberately, into the arms of a neighboring person, in the dark, or blindfolded, and trust to be caught. As Sarah has shown him far more appealing things to do with blindfolds, Sebastian is little interested in the exercise for its own sake, but feels it a useful—if oblique—analogy for his relation to the universe.

Now as to the related issue of the ground being there to greet one's feet, Sebastian knows, rationally, that this can be counted on, for every other person that ground will be solid, yet he feels himself mysteriously, irrationally exempt: that even if

122

every other waking person walks from bed to bath to window or where, *he* may instead find himself stuck with feet dangling into the void, no longer in protected realm of sleep: horizontal, yet eluded by verticality. He would be hard pressed to explain it to anyone, but feels it strongly. He wouldn't mind arguing it with Aristotle, chap 8, "Let us explain again that there is no void existing separately, as some maintain." Such ideas perhaps lend themselves more suitably to written discourse.

Today's adventures alone—and not yet concluded—would provide ample material for a philosophical, if not Aristotelean, meditation. Or poetic treatise? For years the idea of writing one has lain not quite dormant in his brain, and he means to address it; fully intends, in the near future, to act upon it. Just before he took up with Sarah he was organizing the time in his mind, planning to set aside two or three evenings a week. Why, the very day they became lovers was circled on his calendar—now for the other reason. But the relationship has distracted him from his ambition. As their mutual enthusiasm is time consuming (although to Sebastian it often seems their lovemaking inhabits a realm outside time—see Aristotle), the image of himself (of which he is fond) quill in hand, elegantly scratching Mont Blanc fountain pen nib against acid-free paper until the wee hours, is no closer to realization than before. No passion in history has sustained this degree of intensity; it will have to abate eventually. And although the prospect of diminution saddens him—it is in fact too abstract at present for him to invest sorrow in—he has, as prepackaged consolation prize, the aforementioned image, and the prospect of actually putting his mind to the task. There is also the hope that, if pitch of ecstasy must diminish, tension, its negative corollary, might follow suit, might make for a smoother marriage in that case.

He knows he has it in him: a book. At least words. For he knows he knows how to impress with words; so many have remarked; though perhaps here, it is really the accent which seduces: surface. Sarah would reduce him to that, sometimes. But in him is more. He knows there is more, for the world inside Sebastian's head is something wondrous, perhaps as great as any masterpiece Sarah would study, certainly far greater than all of her compositions combined—at least what she's done so far, what he's seen. It is complex and intricate (his world) even what Sarah would call magical; yet ever-inchoate, it eludes his grasp, since occasional scribblings in a notebook, even with Mont Blanc fountain pen, amount to little. Nothing in comparison to the great work he will eventually produce. Before he's forty would be best. Forty-five at the latest. No, it should be forty, really. In any event, it will, it would, be impressive. Something talked about, written about; something not everyone could read. Yet not impenetrable.

But how to harness the myriad impressions? Trying to record any single one, he feels foolish. Yet only the total effect of all the intricate interaction would stun; how to achieve that? For instance, the statue in some Italian church. The single gentle purple shaft of light through stained glass on the white marble female form, like a beautiful scar directly across the noble sculpted nipple—rhyming with, months later, Sarah postured in a certain way, receiving exactly such a shaft of identical color via the prism she had hung in the bedroom window. Where in an essay—or for that matter a novel, sermon, libretto—is a place for such perceptions: these things which haunt him but add up to nothing? Unless, of course, one were to write an autobiography. But one must be significant first. Who would wish to read the life of someone who wasn't? A very exceptional autobiography—exceptionally well-written, that is—might, in a certain sense, be a short-cut to significance. If it were . . . impressive. For what would be the point of putting so much indelible ink, then type, to archival quality bond, if not to impress?

Perhaps he lacks confidence. If only he could learn that from Sarah, who seems to find no idea too trivial, too whimsical to invest her energy and craft. She is, he grants, hard-working; though what she calls work seems to him play: somewhat but not altogether different from kindergarten fingerpainting. Qualitatively different from this world of words, painful articulation of concepts: rendering what the mind's eye sees. It is no surprise the corporeal world is more seductive. A hypothetical body of work seems remote indeed compared to Sarah's exquisite form, which would appear to fluctuate between nubility and ripeness—a cycle that must be his perception, but he could swear objective—perhaps depending on her mood. She has such powers, he believes, just as she changes hair color or style on whim. "I always know the truth," he tells her, "when I behold the coiled threads of your burning bush and see spun gold upon the sheets; only someone bold as you, love, would dare to be copper in proximity to pink. How anyway did redhead genes land in your chromosomes?" "Irish grandmother," she winks. "Ah, yes, S o' Z."

Yes, Sarah, to Sebastian, is exceedingly concrete, and when his mind rises toward her, there is a corresponding ineluctable physical tropism that is utterly straightforward. And that is why, at least partially why, he can lie in her arms in the bed, atop or beneath the quilt she made, in the room with hangings and objects all of her choosing, some her creating: the room he would have to strip bare if she left him—sometimes feels she's made too much her own—yet likes the touch she has, the way she's fixed the place; at odds, alas, sometimes, with his idea of order. But surrendering some order is not the greatest sacrifice, he supposes, to have this unprecedented experience, of lying in another's arms and feeling, for moments at a time, nearly secure.

The daily eruptions which constitute a threat to that precious security seem to Sebastian unbearable blows, blows from which he knows not how to shield himself. Is he instigator? Catalyst? He knows he sometimes is. As often as she'd claim? He wouldn't think; often thinks, in fact, she goads him on; sets up the conversation so he has no choice but to displease her. And then appeasing her can take up hours; oh why is it these patterns can't be broken? Why is it one's greatest solace is as well the arrow in one's side? The gender business is what he finds most trying; she will find it everywhere, and then he's no defense. Perhaps if he had close male friends, there would be more balance; he'd find himself less frustrated, less invested. Often he finds male discourse more—dare he admit?—intellectually satisfying. One oughtn't generalize, of course. Yet female companionship—and not just the sexual—is the draw. Those have been in his life the strongest connections: vaguer word than he is wont to use. (She, when once she saw him spell, pursed lips, wagged slender mocking finger, set its tip upon the "x," and cried out, "C. B., can this be a spelling error?")

Yes, she can play with him—and as we know, Sebastian doesn't mind; not when it's only play. But when she's nasty . . . is it fair that only he is held accountable for similar transgressions? And if he tries to draw attention to this double standard, she will just dismiss him (what she claims he does to her) by saying, "Let's not bring up double standards," opening a whole new category of familiar accusations that bring them further and further from reason, prompting him to call her, perhaps, "my dear misologist,"—with genuine affection.

She does not care to wear this label, is only made more angry by the tenderness; and he cannot forget the recent incident in which she snapped, "Better a misologist than a misOGynist."— utterly ungrounded accusation, conveniently cast any time a female thought process is scrutinized and found wanting—then after uttering, leapt from the bed (a kind of blasphemy itself; there should be a rule against arguing in, even on, their bed) and slammed the door behind her.

Tracing her to the locked bathroom door—sometimes he finds her weeping there after they've fought—he elicited no response and so returned to the barren bed—his body reading mental as physical exhaustion—and napped. His bladder's urgency when he woke dictated he demand entry; and ready to beat upon the door he was surprised to find it open and her gone from there. Sarah's presence, however, was manifest by a rather sinister mobile employing symbols and letters: the symbols for male and female, and the Italian word "orologio" above which stood the letters OB GYN, with the B in brackets. The O GYN, it seemed, meant to parallel the OL OG of the Italian word, and before each was the abbreviation for an unmarried woman, both abbreviations, but MISS was crossed out, whereas MS was not. An altogether muddled contraption, in his opinion. (Whose jokes need footnotes, Sarah?) Even more incoherent than most of her improvisations, but clearly meant to be commentary on their conversation. Then he saw it: the IST. As if throwing a German verb into the jumble of visual syllables needed no justification; he so wished she'd leave language out of her art. Wasn't exploiting him penalty enough? At least leave language pure. And of all places, the bathroom. Well, Sarah does know how to get maximum mileage from any space. And deliberate, no doubt, even if "spontaneous": to choose the space in which distinction between male and female is most directly manifest.

And so, those moments of quasi-security tend to burn or melt away; yet, phoenix-like, return. Back and forth. She likes me, likes me not. Tolerates. Not. The same words under other circumstances might have amused her. Just her mood; there's no predicting. Just as now, there is no way of knowing whether the seamstress is engaged in some frivolous irresponsible activity, or if some dire fate has befallen her. Has she got herself killed in some accident, of which when he learns he will feel ashamed to have complained of inconvenience? Just as with his mother when he was small, and she was invariably late to fetch him at some function or other, he never knew how to think: whether to be all bothered or worried. Often when she did arrive he was fearful to drive with her in that state—so what was the point of hungering for her arrival?—a state he did not entirely comprehend. Very early on he found it entertaining to experience the sensation of riding bumper cars at an amusement park. But later, when he recognized what danger was, the annoyance would transform into terror, that this time she really had got herself killed and he would be orphaned, half-orphaned. He played a game, not shared with his dad, to prepare himself as he stood waiting: he'd try to feel himself an orphan for a half then a whole minute, like holding one's breath and trying to increase capacity. Generally she would arrive by the time he was drowning.

One of Sebastian's greater adult fears is to go out for cigarettes—well, he doesn't smoke them—still he thinks of it that way, that sort of errand—or butter or tea, and find himself in hospital; that is, if he's left nothing talismanic in or on the oven to guarantee return: thus the mundane is transformed to the grand scale of life and death. Now, has this woman landed herself in hospital—there's one very near—and this sign then here for weeks; left, in a sense, to rot? Far worse than posters for an event already past, as they are usually covered with posters more relevant, recent; one can perhaps see their edges, just a hint, like memory. He imagines the sign covered with page after page of revisions: what would be the opposite of tearing pages off a calendar: BACK IN TWENTY, BACK IN THIRTY, BACK IN FORTY-FIVE. BACK TOMORROW, NEXT WEEK, NEXT YEAR, BACK NEVER, GO HOME, DON'T WASTE YOUR BLOODY TIME. It serves her right, he thinks— and is immediately ashamed—if she's got into trouble when she takes time off she shouldn't have; she should have been available for customers. Of course had it been in the vicinity (the accident) there'd be no issue of uncertainty. Someone would have heard the crash, seen the problem (mishap, abduction); local reporters already on the scene; but no, there is only this miasma of uncertainty, and these unctuous strangers with whom he will again be forced to chat. Worse than the telephone which occupies only one's mouth and ear: there is still some privacy; one need not surrender all.

At this moment Sebastian sees, perhaps two blocks off, a wedding, just completed. Erupting from the doors of a church of uncertain denomination are bright guests, motley, then a smear of some silly pastel, lavendar—something Sarah would never choose for her bridesmaids as she plans to design, more likely is in the process of designing the dresses herself, and to make her own gown. He jokes that it's her excuse to delay the event. "No, Seebee, that's your projected wish." Ah, now he sees the shorter dark smudge leading to the unmistakable single blotch of black and white, ever-melded. (The melding he's no trouble with; the ever is what gives him pause, makes him anxious.) From here they might easily have fallen off that bakery cake, perhaps the very cake they will be cutting presently; guiding pieces into each other's mouths while jeering hordes look on. Oh, the thought makes him nauseated all over again.

If he stands still, the wave may overwhelm him; he must persevere. He must be nearly . . . somewhere. If he is not careful, he will wind up a facsimile of some unsavory street tramp, huddled in a corner, against some building. He may look alarmingly like one already, having had no opportunity to refresh himself after that first session of abuse. It is probably as much his disheveledness as his obsessive quest for the tailor that keeps him from peering too deeply into any particular shop. The perpetually present comb in his pocket would do little to repair the damage, and he hardly has the energy to grasp it, as if his hands were not the prehensile appendages they were designed to be. By whom? Some monkey, some god, some fluke?

If he had any food, it would have to be fed him, spooned into his mouth by some charitable hand. He sees the doctor, the pediatrician, moving his mouth; his mouth is instructing Sebastian to say *ahhh*. Sebastian says, dutifully, if half-heartedly, *ahhh*. The tongue depresser presses down: a foreign body in a sensitive realm. Wider, open wider. *AHHH*, but he can't open wide enough. The beige, emery-board-like stick becomes as broad as his tongue itself; it's a shoehorn: cold, metallic; the piece of cake a soft, squat tower leaning toward him, and every time he nearly clears it, it grows another tier until it's the whole matrimonial monument again, uncut, and he can't. Can't possibly accommodate, and a wave of irrevocable eructations ensues.

If he could find a phone along this route, he would ring her, his wife-to-be; too far to call; give her ring. Mind, do not turn on me now. She is good to him when he is ill. Does not ridicule then. She'd come fetch him somehow, take him from this suffering. Of which she was origin? Eve's apple; yellow paper? "Poor little Sea Bass," she might croon, knowing his father called him that: appellation she reserves for tenderness: "Darling Sea Bass, afraid to get wet? Afraid to ride it?" He sees himself a small glimmering creature, amidst an expanse of undulating blue-green. Then he's flapping frantically, as if breath were suddenly conscious, labored, as if his organism were no longer adapted. He opens his mouth. The shoehorn contracts into narrower metal: sharp, curved, some segmented creature dangling from it. He remembers Mum with the can of Spam: "you must eat something, lovey," but he knows he'll gag. He's pierced just trying to sustain himself, his guts excised; the vomit turns blood, the crystal turquoise liquid all clouded with the deep red, almost purple ink.

Oh, he cannot go on with this worse than wild goose chase; he has not the strength. He hasn't the will. His former determination is reduced to veleity. Why is she obsessed with the martyrdom of the stupid saint he wants no part of? Why did he get up today? Nothing has happened. Yet so much, in a sense, has transpired; for this protracted waiting makes everything seem, paradoxically, to accelerate: time speeding up while slowing down. It reminds him of the flip books Sarah makes, starting out with cards, each laboriously marked to represent one or one part of a gesture: one instant of movement in a sequence. To make it become animation, the drawings are rapidly snapped, like shuffling a deck, and then there is narrative. She made one in honor of their lovemaking; in it a man and woman progress through every stage of an act of love. She has several versions, in fact: curiously tasteful depictions; a marvel that nobility of line might be preserved in what is essentially cartoon. The constant in each is the implied ambidextrousness of the simplified female figure, whose hand, right or left, depending; even in the simplified drawings, is visibly loyal to the specialized task of cupping something fragile and timorous; nurturing something hidden from view.

The cards take life through a synthetic speed, imposed motion; what, then, manipulates the physiological—or is it cerebral—pacing which Sebastian is experiencing? Elsewhere in Book IV: "When, therefore, we perceive the 'now' as one, and neither as before and after in a motion nor as an identity but in relation to a 'before' and an 'after,' no time is thought to have elapsed, because there has been no motion either. On the other hand, when we do perceive a 'before' and an 'after,' then we say that there is time ... Hence time is not movement, but only movement in so far as it admits of enumeration."

He thinks of a whole life's landscape, experienced in dream, a dream that might fill only a minute of actual, objective time. It's anxiety's speed, he supposes, now; like increased heartbeats inside the spacious slow silence of dread, caused by some sensory messenger: strange footsteps or such? Some external distortion to cause an equivalent internal one. Does wish he'd taken a course of physics, anywhere; now too late of course.

"Just as the moving body and its locomotion involve each other mutually, so too do the number of the moving body and the number of its locomotion. For the number of the locomotion is time, while the 'now' corresponds to the moving body, and is like the unit of number."

No sense regretting what one hasn't done. But any fool can see he may as well have slept in today, have simply said, to hell with responsibility, with business trips, with being well-groomed, with professionalism; like this woman, an immigrant herself, but obviously all too acclimated to American slackness. How he would love to tear off the scribbled sign, vivid in his mind, and maul it with his feet, expending the last reserves of energy. "Dying man," he sees the headline, "crumples sign, tears, eats, spits it out upon the pavement." But he has too much respect for language, even as it betrays him. Is that nobility, is that faith, Padre? Not your kind, perhaps, but some variety; is that stupidity? As if there were still in the scrap of paper some potential to fulfill the promise that for all practical purpose no longer has relevance.

If he had the car, if he was in his XJ6, he would not feel impotent; he's not used to this going about on foot. But one must, of course, if one wants to get close up to things. He's not sure he could find it now, in its parking space, though he's good with directions; good enough, for someone with training in literature. It's only the day's been so disorienting, to the degree that he's unsure of how to get back to the tailor's. Why, she might be there this moment behind the counter: efficient, apologetic, with his trousers like a proudly displayed newly-snagged fish no longer resisting the reel, his trousers held high on a hanger in her hand, neatly pressed. (Photographers snap the picture of the diminutive Asian woman bearing instead of the largest ever, the longest ever awaited catch—that's how it would be worded.) Or she with uninflected voice might report, "Mr. Sebastian, I so sorry; these yours? I just found." No, no. Not bloody likely.

Far more likely she is still at large. Even as he's ready to curse her, he arrests the anger, for he fears there is at work here some elaborate cosmic scheme to induce guilt; she might be, for instance, with her children (has she children?) in some emergency circumstance. Yes, that could very likely be the case: not that she herself is in hospital, but that she was summoned to attend a critically ill child; what could be more natural, more noble than a spontaneous act generated by maternal instinct? How could he express anything but approval for this valiant hypothetical gesture, detrimental though it be to his trousers? It is perhaps some curious inversion of his anxiousness for Mum, or for himself, when he feared orphandom? Some projected protective fantasy? He's simply jealous, perhaps; for the tailor's very absence, according to this scenario, is indication of her being in the place where Mum was not.

But what would he know of parenting? Motherhood. Of juggling it with career: the issue with which nearly every woman seems obsessed. Thank God he and Sarah have no children, though he would like, when he works out some . . . issues; and Sarah wants, claims she wants, when she is "ready." It's all maddeningly indefinite sometimes. What are her intentions? Their inconclusive banter: provocative, unsettling, rarely provides a clue. The subject of her art is always touchy; nonetheless he attempts to probe, such as the time he found her studying plates of Siennese Madonnas, by Lorenzetti and others, and she shared with him her impressions.

"What I'm really interested in," she said, "is the relationship between their expressions. This is a kind of wimpy Christ child, while this one's more playful. And here's a tender one: wise, compassionate. See, he's touching her veil, as if he's saying, 'Do you know what you're getting into?' A mother/child reversal sort of thing. Can you see it?"

"I see the images, Sarah. I'm not sure I see exactly what you see."

"Oh, Sebastian, try to. Look at these Annunciation ones then. In some she looks really scared, shocked even; other ones she's calm and accepting. Do you like this one by Martini?"

"Like it? Yes, of course, it's art. Real art."

"I love that gold lettering for their speech; it's like some elegant cartoon."

"I would have thought there to be a qualitative difference between Renaissance painting and cartoon."

"O dear Bastion, do you have to be so . . . so literal? See how the Virgin is suspicious; she's frowning, trying to shield herself from the words by drawing her deep blue cape around her, like the words are cold to her. But she's optimistic, in a way, saving her place in the book. And instead of a column between her and the angel, there's a big gold vase of flowers."

"Sarah."

"Yea?"

"Isn't it so that women's creativity is epitomized—traditionally, that is—in the procreative?" Much to his surprise, she did not take offense, though she paused much longer than is her custom before replying.

"You know I think there are all kinds of creativity. Men's

and women's creativity. But it's true that women have that special potential of bearing children, and I've been thinking lately that it probably would be one of the most . . . profound creative experiences." She seemed a bit nervous, out of character; she started to poke at a piece of cardboard with her exacto knife, before inquiring, "What do you think, Sebastian? In a year or two, should we try?" She seemed quite serious; he tested it.

"But you'll have to produce something more original than an ordinary baby, eh, love? A green baby, perhaps? Or polka-dotted?" "An ordinary baby'll do just fine," she said, "because I plan to tackle everything in art before I turn to nature. I'll have exhausted originality, in that sense." Extraordinary at times: her hubris.

"At the rate you're progressing, that may indeed be possible. Spare you worrying over the infamous biological clock. Besides, isn't your Biblical ancestor the woman who managed to conceive when all had given her up for barren?"

"You get an *A* on this quiz, Sebastian. I'm amazed you'd even consider my tradition, that I have one too. Sometimes I feel like I'm just some product of pop culture to you, something that came out of a cereal box one day . . ."

"Sarah, really; what's brought this on? Besides, you'd hardly be product of anything, devotée of process that you are. It's you who's told me time and again product is not nearly as important."

"But you still don't get it, I don't think: that my art, my creativity, isn't some fossilized entity on the walls of a museum or between the covers of a book. It's fluid, active. Orgasmic. You can relate to that, I know."

"Touché. And anything you do, love, as far as I'm concerned, is orgasmic." He knew he could please her by speaking this truth. Even her smile excites him: the lush full mouth. In spite of himself, though, he takes back that pleasure, consistent with their routine: "I'm not so dense that I can't understand the concept of perpetual creation. And if accomplishment is dependent on quantity, you will most certainly have tackled everything in art."

"Ever the master of the left-handed compliment, Sebastard. Why don't you finish the sentence, say what you mean? Quantity rather than quality, right? That's what you're implying."

"You're inferring."

"You must know that your pedantry is a defense, Sebastian."

"Perhaps I require in my life certain immutable standards, in contrast to your own credo, 'what is is always changing.' "

"You're the one who resists the idea of getting married."

"How is that relevant, if you please? And may I remind you that we are engaged; is that resistance?"

"That is a formality. I'm talking about . . . behavior. And what goes on . . . inside you."

"The latter is surely a subject on which I am the exclusive expert."

"Yes, it is, and I wish you would instruct me in that sometime. That's something I want to know.

"Alright, at this moment, what I'm thinking is whether your wish to have a child might also be 'in process'—some fleeting whim."

"It might be in process, but it's hardly a whim. And you know, Sebastian, you have fluctuations too. Sometimes the things you say to me in bed are so beautiful, so meaningful. And then when we have these other conversations, I have to wonder if I dreamed them. It's like a beautiful fireworks display, that stuns you, but what's even more amazing is how it disintegrates before your eyes."

She can be poetic at times. He'd flatter himself, he supposes, to credit his own influence.

"For all I know, your body might be telling the truest story, coming toward me and retreating at the same time."

Always she must pick on abnormalities, his secret flaws, to make him feel all the more exposed.

"Ambivalent."

"Sarah, you know I'm self-conscious of that; furthermore, not everything in life is metaphor."

135

"I'm not absolutely sure that's true either, but tell me something, Sebastian."

"If I'm able."

"Do you want to be a father?"

His silence is not a withholding, not conscious resistance to sharing, disclosure. He did not expect the simple question to overwhelm him. He wants to say it seems a simpler relationship than their relationship, that he might do better as father than as husband, but at the same time, has great anxiety that he would cause anxiety, as he was caused, by his own fumbling father, who in that role was clearly superior—and Sebastian had to balance the guilt with the gratitude, thinking of Mum with the short end of the stick.

He would prefer not to have known; prefer his father had not made the irregular pilgrimages to his room, transformed into some sort of travesty of a confessional by the nature of those visits: his own father seeking a vicarious absolution from the innocent, inexperienced lad who could not possibly transform himself into a surrogate heavenly father (such would require a miracle grander than Catholic transubstantiation—not even the chaplain, the Padre). What might he have said, after all? "The earth, dear Dad; it will not likely cease to turn," before he knew the sentiment himself. All Sebastian could say, with the weight of his father: intimate but oppressive against his little legs under the covers, toward the whispered wrongs: single infidelity; single blow when Mum once again enraged him with some persecution in her besotted state, was "Dad . . . why?"

The initiation of question, received as completed one, merely drew out Dad's monologue: his guilt, all the lame but understandable excuses; causal chain leading to actions assumed by him as challenged by this tiny God: explain yourself? Defend yourself? No, good God, no; the little Sea Bass was only trying to ask, "Why . . . are you telling me this? Please don't reveal these things I wish neither to hear nor understand"—though all that could be summoned into speech was the likewise whispered, interrogative protest intended as plea: the single ambiguous syllable. Why.

Is he any more adept, ultimately, at communication now than then? With so much more of language at his disposal, his command? Can he clarify? Say simple words, like yes or no; I do; I will? That's the thing about social discourse; that's the problem. One can't revise it, as one could a statement made with pen and paper—though pen and paper, Sebastian fears, might prove equally problematic for the opposite reason: their potential to get precisely right the thing one wants to express. And what if one could never realize such potential? Might one be endlessly scratching to the point of harming the finely crafted golden nib? Hardly a pretty sight: row after row of scratched out words; lines, moving further *from* instead of closer *to* refined articulation. She'd say the pretty doesn't matter; she'd say his Mont Blanc's just for show: an instrument of vanity; whereas he would claim it is a tool related to tradition, to ritual; for who, after all, could imagine any great English poet creating a work with the title of Bic? Well, an American poet; some American scribbler just might find perverse pride— But she'd regard his precious writing instrument in tandem with his Rolex: some bourgeois ostentation, affectation; not a twinning linked to order and aesthetics.

No, for Sarah these two properties are mutually exclusive, it would seem. The chaos when she first moved in distressed him greatly; though it was he who pressured her to join him—as she frequently reminds him. He'll never forget the darkroom in the kitchen: chemicals beside the food; trays in the sink where he washes the dishes until they make the sound he loves to elicit from their singing rims and which she, even if she were so inclined, could neither elicit nor appreciate. "Sarah, a kitchen has one purpose, which must by all who use it be respected; otherwise life is simply too uncivilized."

"But Sebastian . . ." She was ebullient as ever that day: radiant, smiling at him, standing on a chair to wrap her arms around his neck, her eyes like green tinted glass. "I just heard from Lisa about an exercise they give women who have trouble having orgasms . . . with men, that is. The woman lies on the bed masturbating, and the man stays in the kitchen."

"Role reversal, is that it?"

"No, no; more interesting than that. The woman takes as long as she needs, in the bedroom, while the man moves from room to room, getting closer to the bedroom."

"During a period of how long? Minutes, hours, days?"

"It just depends, I guess. Probably takes a few tries before he gets all the way to the bedroom."

"Depends on the size of the house, then."

"Kind of surprises her is the idea. Doesn't it sound like fun?"

"Given all that choreography, it seems to me they might just as well perform their calisthenics in the bedroom. Besides which, that is most certainly not an affliction relevant to you, now is it, love? You represent the other extreme."

"I wonder if she's blindfolded."

"Sarah, if you fancy erotic activity in the kitchen, I've no objection; anywhere in this apartment, anywhere you please, your wish is my command, but I hereby decree that the darkroom must find a new home, is that clear?"

In literal obedience, she moved the apparatus to the bathroom, considerably smaller; paraphernalia atop the toilet and such, processing paper, emerging images hanging from clothespins across the shower, beside the hot water bottle she employs to acidify her mysterious female interior. "Must you meddle with the pH of my favorite environment, Sarah?" "Just keeping things hospitable for you, Sebastian. You weren't very happy that time I had to keep you out for a few days; insisted I at least let you insert the little tablets. Didn't they look like arrows?" One could never know with Sarah; given her attitudes and ideas concerning what is life and what, art, it might be some sort of installation meant to merge these two ostensibly unrelated realms. But he simply could not, would not, tolerate it: the clutter; not after the first few weeks, during which they were principally in the bedroom anyway. After that he insisted, "You go rent yourself a studio, love; I don't care how much rent, or where, but home is not where the art is. I need at least semblance of order." Thus Studio Z was born, and he was only too pleased to be spared the searching, deliberating, planning and renovating; to have his relationship to the place remain exclusively financial. If it served her needs, that's all he wanted.

But even when it ceased to function as darkroom, the bathroom was, to Sarah, far more than a merely "functional"—in the ordinary sense—space. All her various cosmetic transformations were performed there. Nor was its scarce square footage an impediment to togetherness, in her mind. Frequently she insisted they be witness to each other's rituals; or, whenever possible, perform tasks for each other: cleaning their teeth, for example, flossing not excluded. "Sarah, do you find it romantic to insert waxed thread between these narrow crevices? Is there something perhaps sexual in easing in and out, over and over? Is there, oh phallic jaguar?"

"Sebastian, you're not being very thorough with mine. If you talk, you can't concentrate."

"It's hardly on the order of brain surgery. I'll do better." He ceremoniously unwound from his fingers and disposed of the thread, scrubbed his hands in the sink, and donned a white robe she had flung across the hamper. Rolling up the not nearly long enough sleeves, he inspected each tooth, fingering each surface, imitating a physician's manner, before taking up, once again, the little plastic box to extract another thread. Though clearly amused by his antics, she persisted in instructing him.

"You have to go a little way into the gum on each side, the dentist told me. Let me show you."

"Tell me, miss, do you find yourself excited while with the dentist, as some women, allegedly, are, at the gynecologist's?"

"My dentist is female, C.B. I mean, Dr. Bowen."

"Well, you're a broad-minded sort."

And so on. Their usual banter. But more peculiar was the tine he watched from a distance as she mouthed syllables at the mirror, a pencil in her hand, rendering, seeming to stop herself in mid-word. A self-portrait, he wondered? Some curious documentation? Scoring the choreography of speech?

"What's this about?" he asked, appearing behind her and hiding her mirrored eyes with his hands. "A series of studies of the most voluptuous mouth on the planet?" But after she pried his hands away and continued, he saw there was little of the narcissistic—alas—in her expression, her intense scrutiny more clinical. Suddenly she turned to face him:

"Sebastian, you're distracting me."

"But I'm not saying anything."

Usually she is pleased, even if she might feign annoyance, to be interrupted by his praises, demands, in fact, his presence. One of their favorite games is to have words, at first unsolicited foreign bodies, evolve into gesture, a tacit pact they have, that no matter what the other is doing, the activity will never preclude receptivity to the other's desire, desire will become mutual, whether it be in the midst of eating, speaking on the telephone (the only time Sebastian finds that activity bearable), reading. "Can't you see I'm busy?" is code for "try a little harder." Usually. What is different in today? he'd asked himself.

"I find it odd, Sarah, that you don't fancy my voyeurism today, you generally love being watched." She was speaking some nonsense into the mirror, freezing her expression at intervals to make marks on the paper. It annoyed him that she was having meaningless dialogue with her other self instead of with her significant other: himself.

"You let me watch you perform all sorts of tasks." He does not care to be excluded: the principle of the thing. She should at least be consistent. "Shall I enumerate?"

"No, Sebastian, please. I won't be that long, if you just let me concentrate. I've never done this before, and it's for something important. For my art, a special project. O.K.? You'll see eventually."

Even now, he has no idea what she was up to that day; but then, if he could understand everything about his inimitable fiancée, she would be some other woman altogether: not the one under whose aegis he could insert himself into the Guinness Book of World Records on the basis of frequency and duration of certain universal acts. Nor, on the other hand, would she be the person he more than occasionally wants to strangle. But he mustn't let himself be distracted, thinking of these personal matters. It's what she does to him so often: he'll be mentally gnawing over some ridiculous, nonetheless excruciating, issue, something connected to Sarah, and suddenly find the sun setting, or rising, a business venture aborted, some idea forgotten, a series of numbers hopelessly muddled—for God's sake, it's Sarah who's got him into this cock-up right now; yet he has little confidence that she will be the one to get him out. He must get himself out. He must act.

He is sick to death of vigilance, caution; of searching. Not only has he no notion of the time; he has begun to feel his own perceptions may be unreliable. Staring, as he has been now for —is it hours?—into every window and door while trying to attend to every fellow pedestrian lest he overlook the woman he may not even recognize has been, to say the least, a strain. He cannot help but think of Aristotle's exploration of the notion (in the larger sense) of time, following the discussion of the void, in the *Physics*: "First, does it belong to the class of things that exist or to that of things that do not exist? Then secondly, what is its nature? . . . One part of it has been and is not, while the other is going to be and is not yet. Yet time—both infinite time and any time you like to take—is made up of these. One would naturally suppose that what is made up of things which do not exist could have no share in reality."

The glint of something in a storefront distracts him—or is it Aristotle who's distracted him; no, grounds him, always—and he finds the energy to squint, once again, through glass, at a curious artifact which gives him an uncomfortable sense of déjà vu. It takes a few moments to identify the mobile which hung above the toilet in his own home not so long ago. Sebastian feels exposed, though he couldn't say why. He has no relation to the abstract mish-mash. But he can't decide whether to flee or confront it. He puts his face against the glass. The muddle of letters and languages is no more coherent than the original version—the construction so chaotic, in fact, that it takes a minute to notice the source of the glint that drew him in the first place: hanging from the tail of the symbol for male, is his very own Rolex, or a bloody good imitation of one. Orologio indeed. He'll just see if that's his pilfered property or not. Even if she intended to return it, she might have asked. On the other hand, she is such a mimetic wizard, it could be cast fiberglass or clay or painted papier mâché; who knows what might constitute its imposter? He must find Sarah; all else seems secondary now. She may very well be inside.

He enters what he assumes to be some sort of gallery to find himself standing before a large grainy black and white photo-graph: a crowd scene. One can make out faces, features, excepting one that's blotted out or peeled off so that only the outline of a male form stands out, leaps really, as conspicuous absence. Many ethnic groups are represented, but no clue as to the nationality of the blank person. ERASURE is the title of the piece. Beside it is a smaller "work": a collage employing blue netted material, like a garter; a swatch of white silk; a grain of rice (authentic looking) and in the middle, a piece of green construction paper in the shape of a rectangle. A small red dot, about the size of a thumb tack, is stuck next to the frame; he wonders if it's part of the work.

All he wants is to locate Sarah, but there's no one in the place, no one to ask. What sort of gallery would be left unat-tended? Someone will no doubt return shortly. Ambivalent as he feels toward the objects surrounding him, curiosity finally out-weighs his resistance. There is a stream-lined bronze beast—

rather elegant, actually; all this must be Sarah's work—has she titled it Jaguar? No, after finding a plastic-encased sheet with titles and prices on the unattended desk he sees that the corresponding number reads "After Brancusi."

Removed from the beast is another "sculpture": a crude wire stick figure; no detailing. Suspended from the figure are two transparent light bulbs, tied together by wire at the narrower tapered top, so that the broader bulb part faces down, toward the floor. A piece of paper mounted on the wall instructs the viewer to pull a little silver chain that dangles thinly between the two bulbs. Sebastian, feeling conspicuous though he has no witnesses—he glances again to make certain—does as instructed. One bulb only lights up. The instructions further indicate, in Step Two, that to make the other follow suit, it is necessary to twist the second bulb manually. Sebastian does so, feeling grossly manipulated, blushing severely. A few moments later, both bulbs go out simultaneously, automatically; then the cycle is meant to repeat. The bulbs cast a ludicrous—not to say obscene—shadow against the wall. Sebastian feels a fool. He turns away.

He'll find another room where he can collect himself. Sarah's work cannot fill every nook and cranny of this building. The adjacent room, to his relief is empty; dark. He needs to rest his eyes. But a white rectangle appears on the wall, then words across it: LOVE'S LANGUAGE'S LIFE CYCLE—two apostrophes in a row; already it's chaos. That's sloppy. After the words, which he assumes are title, come a simple cycle of animated images: a fireworks display—the stages of its process. The sequence employs upward colored streaks, to bursts, then smudges, then fainter until there's blankness again. The white is interrupted by the name Sarah Zeidman, the date, and a tiny *c* inside a circle. The cycle repeats several times before the end with copyright symbol; it's rather clever on a certain level; the colors appealing. Without the title he'd be charmed, but he knows that these visual explosions are meant to represent his own promises through her perception.

Following is another film, not animation, of a man and

woman making love—quite graphic, in fact. Sebastian is relieved that the man is not himself, clandestinely filmed, though in a way the thought of seeing Sarah and himself objectively—arouses; others viewing their—embarrasses at least as much. It lasts only a few minutes but all the while, a bit of green is flashing in the upper right hand corner like a visual pulse; it moves toward the viewer, retreats, enlarges, shrinks; has a life of its own. No sound for any of it. Over.

Immediately, a TV screen turns on; there is a video of a man—the same man in the film?—wrestling with a beast whose spots are red. Then the man turns red and the spots are green; the color vibrant, disturbing, like a television set with an ailment. The beast goes transparent and the man is writhing inside its outline. Then the man is still while the beast is wild, and they reverse roles again. The images have an erotic quality that is uncomfortable. Can this be actual footage—or some splicing of . . . ?

No matter; he doesn't need to see anymore. Someone will be at the desk by now. His eyes don't immediately adjust to the light when he returns to the other room and he nearly trips over a wire he hadn't seen before: some kind of mechanism that activates yet another—can one call it—sculpture? This one produces sound effects as well, and so jarring are they that he does—not having been prepared for them—fall. Embarrassing. He recovers his composure as quickly as he can; makes himself erect again, and must resist the temptation to shield his ears with his hands, from the mocking sound which emanates from a synthetic sun, the disc of which is an enlarged—ceramic?—but frighteningly accurate—Rolex watch, and the rays of which are the coiling and uncoiling tentacles of party blowers. The mechanism causes them to respond as they would to a person's breath, to uncoil, go stiff, and make the characteristic noise before each goes limp and coils into itself again. These particular noisemakers, however, have an added feature: as they expand to full length, each bears the words "the ultimate expression." He recognizes the advertising slogan associated with his brand of watch; she's often ridiculed it more informally. Sebastian feels as if someone's pressed an electronic buzzer to his palm in place of a handshake. "What's all the racket about? Hey, are you O.K.?" Could it be Sarah? No, a stranger: a woman who seems curiously derivative of his fiancée; same style of clothing, makeup, hair, but it doesn't quite come off. Too studied, labored, and he's sure the young woman before him could not be completely transformed on the morrow; her present gestalt the only trick she has. How could he have thought, even for a moment, it was Sarah?—though she could easily be some apprentice, perhaps even infatuated with the inimitable one she attempts to, or inadvertently does, imitate. Annoyed as he is by the pseudo-artistic statement which caused him to fall, he feels the familiar rising—tries to suppress it—that summons Sarah within his imagination. And looking at this girl's perfectly reasonable figure draped in likewise provocative yet casual attire reminds him how skilled Sarah is at choosing and designing for her incomparable body. He is intrigued by the game she makes of what she calls apparel, particularly in the bedroom. She incorporates disrobing and dressing both, in the service of foreplay, afterplay; all is play to Sarah, as her purview is essentially one erotic continuum.

She designs her own undergarments, though she does not shun the lingerie he buys her. She seems to love to make him work at getting through cloth to her skin, which is, as he's often told her, his favorite fabric. One day she'll wear around her waist an elasticized band of lace from which dangles satin ribbons ending in metal closures, which in turn beget satin buttons that peek through and secure the silk around her thigh—he is deft with those closures by now. Or he'll find her buoyant breasts incarcerated within some similar contraption of satin and lace; why, sometimes it's like dismantling a machine just to get to her, then get at last inside her. "Can't I open my presents yet?" he will beg. Sometimes when she can't wait, she'll say, "Take off only what is functionally obstructing," and then he has to guess at

what attaches where, often frustrated enough to resort to tearing
with his teeth; she doesn't mind at all. He never thought pene-
trating a partially clad woman could be as arousing, as fulfilling,
as to enclose himself in one completely nude, but Sarah tutors
him in the richness of variation, permutation.

Of course, when he least expects, she'll have on nothing at
all underneath, and surprise him with the giddy immediacy of
flesh. It's overwhelming then, to have direct access to her stunning
self in all its glory. Yet that is Sarah's specialty: the surprise; she
keeps one guessing in a fashion that transforms the cliché.

"I asked if you were O.K.?"

"Yes. Certainly. Fine. And you?"

"Look, I heard a crash, and I just wanted to make sure."

"Pardon, do you work here?"

"Well, I'm working in the gift shop today. I should get back,
actually." Gift shop? Peculiar notion. Rather crass. Does one buy
the outrageously expensive artworks, and then supplement with
trifles on the way out? Cathedrals with their souvenirs to subsidize?
Or what?

"I don't suppose you'd have a clue as to the whereabouts of
Sarah Zeidman, the . . . artist?"

"Oh, I think Sarah's really everywhere." She smiles enig-
matically but not unbecomingly; a certain previously absent animation is achieved through that smile. Clearly his conjecture
was correct and she is enamored of the woman who links them.
She begins to walk back to the shop; he may as well follow. The
gallery is not providing any answers. Her walk is much brisker
than he would have expected; hard to keep pace with her. When
he finally follows her through a door he would have been unlikely
to find on his own, he has to catch his breath. Then he gasps.

"Winded?" She turns, smiles. Even if the question weren't
rhetorical, he would have trouble answering as he stares at a figure
who seems to stare back from ten or so pieces of white cloth,
hanging on a rack. Each T-shirt's front features the pierced saint
in his most effeminate form, standing with his eyes cast wimpily

toward heaven, as if he might be about to clasp hand to forehead histrionically and claim, "My, my, that doesn't tickle." Sebastian touches the image that springs in some way from himself, as if to reconcile his disbelief.

"I—"

"Those? Those silkscreen T-shirts have been one of our most popular items. They go like hotcakes. If you don't see your size, we're expecting a new shipment tomorrow. What is your size anyway? I can help you find it."

"No, please, it's hardly necessary."

"Oh, come on." She is both shy and bold, this stranger, as she regards, then approaches him. "I think you should try one on."

He realizes that this woman could easily enough be a former, present or future lover, not of his, but of his lover. Her manner is somehow knowing. He has far less squeamishness to dwell upon this possibility than that of other male partners. Sarah might propose they all three pool their resources, as it were, in some imagined or actual scenario. The thing is, that although she seems quite open to the idea of some momentary menage à trois, it is inevitably an instance in which she suggests who would constitute the troisième. It's not that Sebastian wants more freedom in this regard, for Sarah offers all the liberation he requires. Why, the only remotely kinky thing he's contemplated concerns those boxes with windows through which one views women who will do "anything you ask." Anything that does not exceed voyeuristic fulfillment, he supposes. But his idea was to reverse that relation, bringing Sarah with him (if women were allowed on the "other" side of the glass), and tell the professional—and hopefully attractive—female, "You watch us." Yet sometimes, he feels a smallness in him when he considers that he has not had, not known so many women, whereas she can, with her infinite experience of the world, proclaim it time to settle down and have no doubts. A man, after all, should be the more experienced— he knows it's silly—just your male conditioning, she'd tell him.

But must one not acknowledge these inherited attitudes? Can they be so simply willed away?

If she were less dismissive, perhaps they would not surface in unpleasant ways, displeasing to her. He feels genuine remorse when he recalls the night that she rhetorically recalled all nights. She'd asked a question from the Seder, that she'd been given the role, as the youngest, to say, every Passover: "Why is this night different from all other nights?" First she insisted the quote was from Shakespeare, sensing, already, his pedantry; she made him guess what she knew he would be ignorant of. It had been toward the close of their first night together; he'd been, he supposes, seduced by her. She had told him there'd been many men, and he, though appreciative of her honesty, and overwhelmed by their experience, felt troubled by the content of the admission, and critical of what he interpreted as her promiscuity. Because it diminished him? Because he is conventional? Oh, he cannot say, but should not have said then, in response to what characterized their eros as exceptional, "That's quite a compliment indeed, I realize, as now I am aware those 'other' nights might well number past a thousand and one."

"You don't receive compliments terribly graciously, Mr. Bowen; I'd rather you said it straight out, what you think of me as. Here, fill in the blank for me: 'Pity she's a ————.' Crossword clue is five letters."

From the very first, then, the tension against the ecstasy, and mightn't he have listened to that, taken it, in her words, as a sign? He also retains an image borrowed from memory in a puzzling and disturbing dream he'd had after their exchange, when sleep was seemingly shallow: the headmaster visiting a class in which they had been reading of Sancho Panza and his mythical wind-mills, and scolding a boy who had "mispronounced" the title. "We do not say Don Kee-hō-tā," the headmaster said sternly; "we say, rather, Don Kwĭks-ot. All repeat please."

"I think this one might do. After all, we want it to be long enough."

"I beg your pardon?" Did she wink at him when she smiled just now, or did he imagine it? He cannot be imagining that she is beginning to unbutton his shirt. Sebastian finds all of this quite confusing; it begins to be hard to separate his memories and fantasies of Sarah, and his arousal, from this disconcerting circumstance.

"I can tell you don't feel comfortable. Why don't you take it over to the dressing room then? Down the hall, back the way we came. And come back to model it for me when you're ready."

"I'm not at all sure I care to try on this garment. Do you understand?" He feels ridiculous holding this banner on a hanger; he wants no part of it. But she does seem determined, and if he leaves her, ostensibly to find these fitting rooms, he won't be standing here, pressured, anxious, any longer.

"You really can't tell until you try it on; trust me. I know it sounds corny, but it's you. It really is." Her eagerness is sweet in a way.

"Where is the fitting room, did you say?"

"All the way down the hall. Just keep going until you can't go any farther."

"Alright, I'll be going then." He starts the journey, and turns back to see her nodding and pointing in encouragement. She'll never know whether or not he puts it on. To do it immediately would be less awkward than carrying it, first held up high in his right hand, then folded over his left arm, as he does now. He has yearned for a change of clothes since morning. Still he can't bring himself to make the substitution. All the way down the hall, she'd said, but as far as he can tell it dead-ends. He sees no rooms: only other hallways. And what became of the artworks? He feels he must have gone a different route than the one he took when he followed her into the shop.

Sebastian finds himself moving down a corridor, facing a stained glass window; immediately he knows whom it depicts. Is it a permanent installation? It is actually beautiful, not at all abstract; it enobles the saint. An image copied from one of the more

149

flattering paintings, he supposes. Appealing to the eye though it is, the image does the opposite of mitigate his dread. O Sarah, why not just make stations of the cross: trials of a single day demarcated; go all the way with blasphemy. It almost seems appropriate. Suffering has seemed to last already an eternity.

Good Christ, he shudders to see himself moving, arrows and all, from station to station: his own brand of deposition; the beating, unto death. No doubt she would do it were he to present the idea; scold herself for not having thought of it sooner. She'd try to convince him it was homage, as well as no disrespect to the historical or mythological figure whose ordeal is traditionally thus demarcated, and to whom her tradition has given no acknowledgment; has in fact erased. He wonders how serious she can be about her own tradition; her relation seems unsophisticated, like an adult's memory of nursery rhymes, fairy tales: sentimental value. When she sings or recites what she recalls from sacred books, Scripture, she cannot even translate into English. How can you understand the meaning, then, he asks, but she insists the meaning is the ritual. That's a meaning he understands as well; it's one of her more cogent arguments, but language; what of language? It must play a part in understanding, must it not? He recalls, with some uneasiness, a poem he began, long ago; showed to the Padre, one Maundy Thursday evening, in preparation for Good Friday. The Padre praised it highly, though it was merely one line. "Such sophistication of language," he'd said. "And theological depth. You must work more on this, lad. No, we've not seen the best of our Sebastian yet." All the same, he could never think how to continue from his opening line: "My eros, hundred-arrowed, lies . . ."

It's paradoxical, that when in aftermath of love, he feels her soft breath upon him, he could almost believe the Padre, enough to proclaim from the rooftops, affirming, "Ladies and gentlemen, I am pleased to report; the earth will not—indeed it will NOT likely cease to turn." But all would take him for demented, hearing peculiar sentiments expressed in archaic language, would ask he at least speak plain English.

The ability to affirm that, during moments such as this when her breath is far from his, seems as plausible as the ability to say "I do," soon to reach practical application. And yet in his rehearsed imaginings, he can't make his way to the second vowel; the sound seems ludicrously long, or round: embarrassing, excessive. Thus he detours: I dare say . . . I definitely may . . . I don't believe it's quite time . . . I do believe I need more time to think. I delegate responsibility to my better half, currently in shadow. I desperately want to say these two simple syllables, Ladies and Gentlemen, but I feel my mouth is clamped with peanut butter; you know the feeling.

Fruits of various kinds, mostly tomatoes, splat against his person, his face, dribbling their innards down his elegant white tuxedo—designed by the bride for her more conservative groom—because he is violating the principle that the show must go on. And such a spectacular show this was billed to be: betrothal of a most unlikely couple; tickets purchased by some merely for the purpose of viewing the bride, renowned for her sexual prowess, in her far from traditional gown—standing room only. And here he's made an ass of himself, spoilt everything.

Wouldn't it be convenient at times, to turn one's mind off? When, after all, is it ever allowed to rest? Not during sleep, surely, when so much intensive imagery is generated: that which she insists he share when they wake, claims to understand better than he. But his own dreams—how could another, better?—even an intimate? She transcribes hers, and sometimes his, into her sketch book. Had he access to that book, might he find studies for this window? This garment? The other works that borrow or imagine his experience? Or might he, worse still, find fragments of language from his own mouth, mumbled in a hypnogogic state; images from his own mind that are foreign to him, incomprehensible, yet served as seeds for her artistic images? He cannot compose himself while in view of this disturbing window, which he feels he ought either to smash or genuflect before. Or would that constitute a masturbatory gesture? He thinks, in spite of himself, of the Eric Gill sculpture, from the Tate Gallery: that Sebastian, modeled upon the artist's own physique. The sensual, feminine smoothness of the stone Sebastian identifies with more than he would like. He has not shown a reproduction to Sarah, though she would be proud to find him in any way receptive to a modern work: something of this century.

Once he gets past the stained glass, he finds, at last, a room, but no evidence would mark it as a fitting room. Almost against his own will, he begins to unbutton his shirt: the task she'd begun. A rectangle of light. This is the same room he entered before then, where the films are shown. Why hadn't he recognized it? The image that the stained glass window borrowed now appears before him, in black and white. Suddenly he's streaked with red lines: tiny rivers from his wounds; then blackness. What is the point? He wants to scream: Sarah, the point, please? What are you trying to prove, and to whom? Among this multitude of works should not one be privileged to speak to the creator, whose ear is always near, no matter where?

The white rectangle again. He is tense, unsteady on his feet; he sits on the single chair that faces it, the only piece of furniture in the room. The next image startles, partly because of its beauty. It is a familiar image, and one with which he knows he has recent acquaintance: the projection of a slide of a famous painting; one which he has seen. Where? Yes, on the trip to Italy, not long after they'd met. Impulsive of him, out of character, to bring Sarah; he'd told her he couldn't spend that many nights without her, but had to do business, couldn't cancel. It felt like a honeymoon of sorts. He remembers being awed by this work at the top of the stairs, at San Marco. He recognizes the two figures who bend slightly toward one another, separated by an elegant column, framed by arches and more columns farther back, that give the painting depth, symmetry. He can respect this image more than anything he has seen in the past hour, for there is no doubt in his mind that this is art, and a welcome surprise in this context; ironic, that it should be surprise. Sad.

He hears a mechanical noise and the image gets larger, closer, as if seen through a zoom lens. The arches cannot be seen now, and the structural, compositional perfection is not as accessible to the viewer, though it is possible to appreciate the detail even more fully. There is nothing haphazard in this work. He is relieved to be reminded that Sarah also appreciates such art—her study, if idiosyncratic, of the Madonnas, for instance. She can't come close to producing art of this quality herself, of course, but she has good taste. That's a start. If she could somehow restrict her productivity, consolidate her influences and ambitions, perhaps she, and he, would be better off. But she's not a charlatan. Not even a dilettante—just a talented girl with an over-active imagination, responsive to an overwhelming number of stimuli. Who, after all, possesses a perfectly proportioned psyche? No one woman can be perfectly proportioned in all ways.

He can begin to collect himself in this serene environment: one exalted image, amongst pure white walls. This is what art should do: offer clarity and tranquility, a kind of order, rather than the opposite. Of the opposite there is more than enough in this world; of that he is today particularly and painfully cognizant. Perhaps that heightened awareness is the reason this moment of composure seems precious. If only creations of this caliber could exist again, ones which foster harmony rather than discord. If there were perhaps patrons again; he considers himself one, after a fashion. And precious little credit he receives.

With a barely audible click, his transforming experience is radically, disturbingly altered; his composure retracted. A horrified Sebastian watches as these same figures—pink clad angel on left, blue virgin on right, remain as they are: still. Against this backdrop of stillness, their lips—upon which his eyes had not thought before to dwell—begin to move. The subtle animation of their painted expressions is replaced by another active sort: audible syllables accompany each opening of mouth. Sebastian thinks of icons which purportedly weep or bleed; miracles, alleged signs; can he be imagining this? No, a travesty. Parody. Sebastian, who has only vestigial and as we know ambivalent relation to religion—and a layman's relation to art—suddenly feels protective toward both, violated on their behalf. He tries to ignore the sound that in some bizarre fashion appears to emanate from their two-dimensional mouths, yet hears all the more acutely the imposed dialogue: "Senta, Maria." Italian, then, is it? Perhaps only the angel will speak; that would be appropriate—if there can be an appropriate within the blasphemous—since the Virgin's function is to receive the message; why need she comment on it? Humility and receptivity communicate most effectively through silence, he would imagine.

He can resuscitate a memory of Sarah and himself viewing the Fra Angelico together, atop the stairway at San Marco, holding hands, when love was virtually newborn. They were silent, respectful, receptive. He'd thought little of it when later she told him, "I'd like to design a dress with just those colors of the angel's wings: scaly rows of burgundy, teal, gold, white, yellow, and the texture of bird wings." The little that he had thought was this: she has an adorable imagination; she can't leave anything alone, always acting on something. But she'd feel such a sentiment dismissive. He'd also thought it sweet when she insisted they make an excursion—"you mean pilgrimage?" he'd asked—to the Catacombs of Saint Sebastian in the Eternal City. It seemed a sentimental gesture, or romantic, like his wanting to take her to London someday, where she could have her hair styled at Harrod's; they would bring her coffee, "do" her nails, call her Madame; things that would amuse her. But would he bring her to the Tate Gallery to see the Eric Gill sculpture, with its strange erotic power, that he feels somehow uneasy to share, thinking also of the man's own complex life, intricate disturbing eros. In the same building is housed the artist's other sculpture, more explicitly erotic, titled *Ecstasy*. The Gallery remained off the agenda.

Why does he recall the feeble English of the French female guide? (He would have understood her better had she spoken her native language.) At the end of the tour of the most popular of the Catacombs—presumably because unnerved by the rudeness of a large group of American and admittedly British tourists (the less rude though) she concluded with the skewed sentiment, "I hope you are very impressioned." Sarah, with her ever-tactile imagination, loves to borrow the phrase, saying, "Sebastian—tonight—make me very impressioned. Mark me." And he, joyously obliging, seals his mouth to her nape, his hands pressed to flesh, then all of him in her as deep as he goes.

Though when she chooses, she'll turn the thing against him, to prod him out of petulance, or simply to provoke: "Have I wounded you, Sebastian, martyr mine?" And he'll retort, "They've not the feel of Cupid's arrows, these." But after he's had his fill of verbal scourging—as if she senses when she's gone too far—she will appear, like a vision, a matter of twenty-four hours at most until she's kneeling before him, penitent: "Sebastian . . ."—softly, as in a confessional—"can saints absolve?" Is it his fate, then, to be both confessor and scapegoat, all because he chose to take the sacrament in adolescence only to renounce before the age of twenty-one? But is it the adopting or renouncing that qualifies him? Moreover, is it privilege or curse?

In either case, what choice has he when she kneels before him, buries her head in his lap? Humble, giving, as always, arousing, she takes great care to hold, just so, the obstinate retracting—delicate as an egg but without the protection of shell, yet unfailingly accommodating with her goodly assistance—and to use the other hand as if it had the range of two? "You be my arrow," she whispers to a part far from his ear: encouragement that leads them both to ecstasy.

Is it further his fate to have ecstasy bound, always, with its opposite? (The analyst might have had a stance on that, had they ever progressed beyond nutrition.) Is that perhaps the case for all humans? —Everyone forlorn after fucking and all that: coitus and tristesse; wasn't it a saint said that? Since the world can't possibly be adequate after a visit to heaven, and since the erotic paradise he and Sarah frequently inhabit is the epitome of exaltation, is it not logical that any post-coital landings could not help but feel a fall? The dizzying vertical distance. He's probably rationalizing. Might one better write about such things—if one were able to arrive at the proper philosophical plane; a higher elevation, to offer perspective?

Will the angel now speak to the audience, he wonders. "Ladies, you can make a dress based on my wings, but act now; call this number for Studio Z"? No, Sarah is not crass. Her intent is not—he thinks not—to defile. She thinks she is making some statement, probably imagines she's in some sense surpassing the Beato Angelico. But why, to Sebastian, does the Virgin look alarmed, paler, as she receives the next statement?

"I will look you right in the eye, Virgin, and I know it will be hard for you, confuse you, but I have a message from on high I must deliver. I think you may already know, in part, although you are obliged to affect surprise; as you are a woman of considerable understanding. I believe you know you were not meant to be ordinary; you know many things. I am not surprised, in fact, to find you reading."

"Angel," interrupts the Virgin's lips, "I would not be so presumptuous—though other images might depict me thus"— Sarah has listened to him for this language, he thinks; it is not her own colloquial melee—"as to place my finger in some page to save a place, for it is already clear to me there is never any going back to that moment. Life has already changed; has it not, Angel?" Sebastian feels, in spite of his resistance, a personal resonance in this question. "There is no point in pretending otherwise."

"Our arms are folded the same," the Virgin continues. Quite

a monologue she's been given. "Our haloes match, gold; but this column between tells the truth. We are more separate than linked, more different than alike. I'm blue and you're pink, but I know you won't make it easy for me: give me a girl, quiet and withdrawn like me. History would not have it. This plan was conceived long before me and I will be humble, grateful, as there is no such thing as choice."

"Senti, Maria; Santa Maria." Now that is ridiculous, to pepper the English with colloquial Italian; make it all one or all the other—subtitles even. Extraordinarily poor judgment. "I am only a mouth, a mouth of the Lord."

"Oh, Angel, how I envy you that, because I am suddenly so much flesh—like the one I will bear. We will have the pains without the pleasures, and be glad in them, grateful for our impoverishment. He is already gone from me, you know, the one who has only begun to be with me, of whom you came to tell me. Yes, I know you are mouth, Messenger. I am holding myself modest like you, in greeting, but I'm frightened, weak. I want to retreat to that dark cell behind us: those bars I'm not sure are shutting me in or the world out—but no matter; it was not to be. It will instead always be you and me: our discourse, admitting just a little patch of world, like the green of this garden. I could be staring at that column, avoiding you; I could shut out your words, your presence. You see I'm almost wall-eyed: how I look half at you and half into the distance. But you fix me with your unrelenting gaze: half wry, half compassionate." The lips of the figures never rest in this peculiar cartoon.

"Maria, I hardly know what to say; there is only this news. It is not for me to counsel."

"There is nothing to say, Messenger. These walls could crumble and my fate would be fixed still, because it is written, and will be depicted hundreds of times, or more, as here in the very plaster that holds up this church. You would still fasten your eyes upon me and I would be as I am, trapped in time. Thousands have frozen my life at this juncture to seal my future: you the mouth, myself the womb. And so it is my honor, Angel. Let my yes that you already knew rise with you; I have always been expecting you: your visit mere formality, but necessary, I know. And now you leave in knowledge that your mission is fulfilled."

By the end it seemed almost natural: the oddness of the putty-like lips gaping at one another. They became an appropriate vehicle for the content, about which he still has grave misgivings, and yet it is one of Sarah's more thoughtful projects, more than whimsical. He would like to discuss it with her. What is the statement, he would ask first off. Does Sarah admire the Virgin Mother? Or is she calling her fool? Presenting her as victim? Or is she expressing ambivalence: what he feels now. He cannot sort out his own responses—certainly not here, and even though he probably deludes himself, he has the sense their discourse might enlighten him. What is she trying to say about her own views, toward motherhood and so forth? Is this a veiled way of saying she's not tempted after all? That it was a whim? This is the first work he's seen of hers which engages him enough to elicit a complex response; a relief to move beyond a programmatic humiliation or annoyance or anxiety.

Perhaps then, he should be seeking the exit rather than alleged dressing room, but the gallery has become a virtual maze in his mind, and any relief from the narrowness of hallway would be welcome. He cannot stay here, though; he must enter the constriction again, so as to press onward. He leaves the room he had not initially recognized, to proceed through the interminable length of corridor. When will he arrive somewhere? It is dark, and he comes upon no artwork to break the monotony; ironic that they could serve as relief despite their own oppressive value. Being outside was exhausting, granted, but the air, at least, the openness—

Sebastian yearns for space, and when he feels he can no longer bear the claustrophobic environment—thinking to himself, three more yards, two more yards, one; three more steps, any second now—he comes upon an opening. He has no wish to peer, be cautious; hence boldly enters but is, again, startled, enough to drop the T-shirt still on its hanger. Get a hold of yourself; you're so jumpy. You might be hallucinating. What had first appeared to be an army of decapitated humans is in fact only mannequins: rows of headless dummies, some clad in pieces of muslin, others draped with brown paper—why does he think of her holocaust nightmares, clinging to history—but a scattered few dressed very ornately indeed.

Closer inspection reveals the intended function of the several elaborate costumes: a function relevant to himself, and one which gives him pleasure. This must be, at last, the fitting room, and Sebastian is delighted to have arrived. He sees the long white gown—is it silk?—whatever fabric it is, there are layers of it, gathered like a Greek tunic, almost austere. Another has quite the opposite effect, with bold angles, a bodice and skirt like pyramids put tip to tip; there is hardly a waist to it. Few other women but Sarah could wear it. The veil is constructed to stick straight up as another pyramid, upside down. Most peculiar. One outfit is composed entirely of Japanese fans: exotic, that. But hard to move in, he'd imagine.

Several of the designs seem to transfer the idea of veil to the body: this tube-like piece, for example, inside a sheer overlay. He finds it quite fetching; would love to get a glimpse of Sarah in that. Variations on the body veil complete the collection. One, naturally, is green, with a sack-like boxy inner part; not nearly as seductive as the previous design, he thinks, until he sees that the inner piece is stitched only in front; it has no back: just the sheer white to drape. Perhaps it is an unfinished piece—unlikely; it would be just like Sarah to annoy and entice him at once, for just imagining her bottom's contours through that diaphanous curtain makes a familiar pressure, which makes him self-conscious, though he knows it's ridiculous, amidst the inanimate bodies. As he's found the fitting room, he may as well put on the much humbler garment that he has carried all this way, if only because he finds his shirt and jacket unbearably constricting and sweaty. Removing both feels strangely liberating; he means to fold them but decides instead to let them drop to the floor. The looser, and mercifully longer, shirt is hardly his "style," but he is surprised to find it comfortable, almost soothing, against his moist skin.

He recalls Sarah telling him of a French designer whose costumes had but two designations: whore or nun, identically scant, identically seductive, differentiated only by absence, or presence, respectively, of a veil. But it's these veils in which he now invests his imagination: the last two variations, which complement one another. Oh, to think of her stately breasts, celestial bodies unto themselves in symmetry: their small delicate aureola each peeking out from behind what is sheer white from waist up; while the last gown is sheer from waist down to allow the radiance of her geometrically transformed sun. Only Sarah would have the resourcefulness to play with color in such a way: not dye in fabric but the natural hue of herself. The white serves as curtain for what is too stunning to be directly viewed: the glorious soft copper triangle.

It does seem a terribly long time since he's felt her thrashing, yielding, or simply soft breathing against him, held by him, holding. When he finds her, he'll tell her everything, without even blaming her for her part in it; he'll be that generous. And she'll say, "That's great, Sebastian, how simply wonderful, my Starburst, because you're still here and we'll have three nights together we hadn't expected to have." Or she'll fall to her knees, begging his pardon for the pain she caused him by her oversight—little yellow piece of paper. "Oh yes, my love, I see how large this little thing became. I had no idea," she'll say. "I'll make it up to you, and accept whatever punishment you choose to assign me." Then she'll make that concupiscent combination of sly wink and lascivious flick of tongue. He will bring his face forward to meet the sensuous organ, mingle his own with it; he will abandon himself to the pale green eyes whose lashes and brows are just a bit darker than the burnished copper mane—never the pale hardly visible lashes of some with that coloring. And as grande finale, she will bare the glorious oxymoronically soft inverted pyramid—what would he ask the oracle?—as radiant, as spectacular as the sun going down, colorist of the sky. More rare than a total eclipse is this sight, nightly his, when mound of Venus, second planet from the sun, is, in paradox, itself the sun. "What is your preference," she will ask, "the sun setting or moon rising?" "Each in turn, if you please," he'll say. And they'll turn and turn and turn: that gradual rotation containing for him more than the sum of all the wishes wished on stars, including his own that resembles a prayer to the Being he wishes he could believe in still, that this transforming of celestial bodies which both grounds and allows him to soar, might it never cease.

He will offer no erudition this night—if he can but find her—take no risks. Why, Sarah, will this night be different from all others? Because I will be different, I will make myself worthy. How simple life could be. He could forget all this anguish of searching for what can't be found. What more need one find than love, after all? How many yearn for it? A crime, in a sense, a sin, if you will, not to recognize such good fortune. He shouldn't take things like the T-shirts personally, that's his problem—if you can't beat join, doesn't his present garment demonstrate the idiom?—that's always been his problem. He must remember that he often reaps the benefits of her overactive imagination. Banish all the ridiculous questions with which his brain is perpetually besieged: worn down, no doubt: its cells, as by illicit chemical substances? Does she love me, love me not? Is it love or is it lust? How many angels can fit on the head of a pin?

"Sebastian, how strange to see you here." Suddenly she's right beside him. "Aren't you supposed to be in the sky?" Then she turns to her "crew": a roomful of actual women, non-mannequins, each of whom, it seems to him, bears some feature of resemblance to Sarah. Yet each different. He finds this disconcerting yet compelling, and watches, mesmerized in spite of himself, as they feed yarn through a cage, pulling strands with their hands like fingers through long hair. They are always in sync with one another, this symphony of weavers, as they lift foot, bring hand forward, place foot down again, pulling each thread by means of a metal implement through what looks like long metal needles. It is strangely soothing to watch as some untangle the yarn or unravel it from spools of every color. He can see that if observing them is calming, to be engaged in this activity might be therapeutic. But whether the product of that activity would constitute a work of art is quite another matter.

The women acknowledge their supervisor with a collective smile and nod. Sebastian feels a pinch. "Cute outfit, C.B. Is that the equivalent of a vanity license plate?" After whispering in his ear she turns again to the women. "And who is working on the tapestry?" All the hands lift in lyric choreography to gesture toward a smaller room off to the side; Sarah moves with her inimitable swift grace. Before he can blink, she's back.

"I think you like it here, Sebastian." She takes his hand in hers and places it on the wooden part of a loom: the part which comes forward in coordination with the weaver's foot. "This is called the beater." She winks and turns to leave.

"Sarah, where are you going? Can't we talk?"

"Where did you come from, seems like a more appropriate question; I could ask you that. But I've got tons of work to do, Sea, you know I load up when you go on your business trips. My job takes discipline too, you know. I guess you could come up with me if you want." He runs after her. What else can he do?

"What happened anyway? Did she stand you up? Cancel at the last minute?" For a woman of sub-average height, Sarah does take extremely long strides.

"No, Sarah, nothing like that. You musn't joke. I have a great deal to tell you." She seems hardly to hear him, intent on examining a series of stained glass panels in various stages of progress. Each room into which he follows her will undoubtedly house a different project. How will he gain her attention? She regards the patterns cut from paper adjacent to large pieces of colored glass arranged upon a wooden table. Then she takes a notched instrument with a little wheel on the end and marks a piece of glass across the middle, places her thumbs over the top of each half, and snaps them apart, exactly even.

"Now you try," she says, handing him the implement.

"But, Sarah, I hardly . . ." She's off before he can conclude his protest, attending to a piece nearer to completion, applying a white substance.

"Flux," she says, raising her eyebrows, placing strong emphasis on the vowel and the final *k-s* sound, to dramatize its similarity to their favorite verb. "So the copper doesn't oxidize."

"Copper musn't oxidize," he repeats softly, touching her hair. Then she is melting thick silver wire with a soldering iron, telling him more disconnected bits of information. "It can bead up, just like mercury." Mercury: that which is contained in a column to offer measure, to serve as an instrument or index or order, but could be ruptured, like some unlucky blood vessel. Hundreds of tiny silver beads might gather mass as they roll, expand into boulders, white cannonballs that splat against him, harder than ice, bruise him; he's knocked to the ground. But in the course of his fall the beads soften, liquefy; become a blanket of silvery snow, into which he sinks: deep, deeper; sinking still.

"But this is the best," she says, thrusting apart the legs of a pair of unusual scissors for him to regard, "the two-sided scissors. They leave a space in the paper pattern, just like the glass will have, so it's an accurate model."

He isn't following. Is she genuinely trying to include him? To share? Or to distract him? Or simply avoid him? He can't tell. He has never seen her in her studio; doesn't know her work modes. Perhaps she is showing off for him, trying to convince him how skilled this labor is. But does she truly believe he would appreciate even the highest level of skill if it were to be applied exclusively toward his humiliation? For there it is, directly before him, his own paranoid vision; one station of his suffering: the beating, in beautiful blue and ruby and gold.

"I wanted that to be a surprise," she says, smiling in all innocence. Ostensible innocence.

"That's partly what I wanted to talk with you about, Sarah; it's quite important. You see, I'm not sure— That is, this mythology you've built around me—at my expense, may I say—I wonder, has it anything really to do with me? Ultimately. What I mean is, perhaps you are aggrandizing me, putting me on some precarious pedestal. I do feel at times a commodity, a vehicle for your inspiration."

"I'm still listening," she calls, but she has already left the room. He must keep his wits about him to keep up with her, not lose her altogether. She's racing up the stairs now. "Answer me this, Sebastian. If you were female and I was male, would you feel the same way."

"Well, I can't answer that, Sarah. We're who we are; our sex is part of who we are, is it not?" He has to stop to catch his breath. "I know that tradition makes woman a man's muse, and inverting the formula is fair enough, I suppose, but I can't help feeling—trivialized—Sarah. Isn't there a lift in this building?"

"There's a freight elevator but it's iffy. We use it for transporting heavy equipment or large artworks."

"I see. Well—trivialized, I think I was saying, or sometimes an even more sinister—do you hear what I'm saying?" She stops on the step and turns to him.

"Look, Sebastian. If you only came here to criticize me, came to where I work to knock my work—I mean, you've never been supportive of my art, and you know what it means to me."

"I think it hardly fair to make such accusations, considering it's I who pay the rent for this . . . space."

"I knew you'd say that. It's just . . . I mean, I appreciate that, I really do. And I only accepted because you insisted. It's just—

there are different kinds of support, and one doesn't necessarily
. . . imply the other."

She begins to climb again; it seems they've been ascending
forever. This vertical travel is making him dizzy and he is relieved
when she stops at a landing, then proceeds through a long, high-
ceilinged hallway. They pass together in front of an enormous
photograph—or a painting so realistic that it simulates one: a
picture of cars, several in a row; red, white, silver, and finally his
own green Jaguar, encircled in red crayon. To the right of the
Jaguar is a painted black +, the symbol used in addition, followed
by a lower case *d*, likewise circled in red. He has to study it to
assemble the pieces of meaning: play on image and language—
sloppy, like a mixed metaphor; but of course the solution is "green
card." Très amusant, Sarah. Oh dear, she has a strong lead again;
fortunately he sees the room she entered; follows.

This room contains rows of desks which sport fang-like at-
tachments. At these desks are both women and men, concentrating intensely as they manipulate small saws, the blades of
which are slender as thread. Gold and silver dust accumulates on
the floor below their toil: an attractive debris. She's in the far
corner like gleaming copper, consonant with the other lovely
substances in the room. Still she stands out, as always. Protective
goggles give her the appearance of an "alien." He oughtn't disturb
her now; she, like her coworkers, is focused, principally upon
what she holds: a hose which projects a long blue and orange
flame. She directs the flame toward a tiny object on a rock—or
what appears to be rock. When she pauses, he moves toward her;
stands a while, uncertain. She senses his presence, for even before
he can speak she cuts him off.

"We can talk tonight, but I'm so busy now, my Starburst,
Sea Bass, Sagebrush." At least she smiles when she glances at him.
"I'll be making the wedding rings here today. Remember Florence?
The streets that might as well have been paved in gold—every
other shop selling it—and we looked at wedding rings even

though we hadn't been together very long—because we thought we might need to pretend we were married if we stayed in some of the smaller villages. Those Catholics."

The memory makes him feel less estranged again. They were indeed far less well acquainted when he asked her to accompany him for those ten blissful days. Yet they were close—became close, in the course of those days and nights. The only argument he recalls was one concerning the restoration of the Sistine Chapel; she found it too bright in its restored state, claimed they ought to leave it be, whereas he, naturally, held the opposing position: "Sarah, how can you find anything negative in cleanliness? Objets d'art need attention like any other, or are they exempt by divine decree from dust and decay?" That is, of course, the thing about Americans. They've no concept of history, no true knowledge of age, of time. "Do you realize, my dear, how old these brushstrokes are? And furthermore, the experts say . . ." How refreshingly trivial—though not unrelated—was that debate in contrast to their current ones.

"Only you would elect to go abroad with a virtual stranger, oh trusting woman."

"I think it was more of a risk for you, my straightlaced seducer." She does have an irresistible smile sometimes.

"Touché, as to straightlaced, but who seduced whom?" Would she remember—of course she would—their language games, in the pensione and elegant hotels: taking clinical sexual terms and making word-play as foreplay, stringing the words together into sentences that would then be uttered while kissing, hearing the vibrations, creating tongue twisters. Whose idea was it? Collaboration, most likely. Her sentence was "A cunning linguist speaks fallacious o's." Then he played with the word lallation while lapping his tongue gently over all of her, her softest parts, lovely hood ornament.

"Sarah, may I give you one very brief exam? A review, actually. Complete for me the sentence, a cunning linguist . . . Of what must one beware?"

Without hesitation she supplies the missing words, at top volume, startling all the previously absorbed metalworkers and jewelrymakers, who look up from their soldering or sawing, then over to each other as if to say, "Well, that's Sarah." Though embarrassed by this attention, he is terribly pleased that she recalls—re-creates—her enthusiasm spontaneously, genuinely. It was a more satisfying honeymoon than most newlyweds ever have, he'd imagine. When, if, they are newlyweds, could they possibly surpass—even approximate—? "My little flame-bearing alien," he says tenderly, barely audibly.

"Sebastian, don't let me get distracted. I have to run and put some things in the pickle."

"Pickle?"

"You can come if you want. There's another kind of beater in there." If she winks through the goggles, he can't perceive it. Given her efficiency, she'll be back before he could get there, wherever "there" is. A smaller connecting room, it appears. In her absence, he examines the pieces that populate this part of the room. Most appear to be ordinary bracelets or necklaces; nothing threatening, unusual in design, but that's a given, isn't it? On one of the "rocks," two flat pieces of silver are soldered together in the shape of a crucifix. He can't resist commenting when she returns: "Funny piece of jewelry for a Jewess."

"Touché to you," Sarah replies, and adds, "You know I play seriously. And this martyr theme has taken me into all kinds of new territory."

Under his breath: "Both of us, I fear." He notices for the first time the earrings she is wearing. (Her lobes are thrice pierced; today there are two "vacancies.") Through one hole on each side is fastened a silver rectangle with three tiny arrows, all pointing different directions.

"Sarah, tell me something. Will a time ever come when you feel you've exhausted this . . . material? Ready to move on to something else, some new thematic focus?"

"Yes. Definitely." Her simple affirmative takes him completely off guard, and for some reason fills him with foreboding, whereas he had anticipated feeling this same way in response to the opposite answer. He does not want to pursue the issue, now that he has raised it; it makes him uneasy, feels too close to the void. He reroutes the conversation; anything to remain engaged with her.

"You wouldn't, by the way, know the whereabouts of my Rolex, would you?"

"You accuse me of making illogical leaps in conversation? Isn't that called a non sequitur, Sebastian?"

"We were speaking of jewelry."

"Is that dumb bourgeois watch all you care about?"

"I love you, Sarah."

"Sebastian, you're not making sense. You like to make sense. Are you deliberately trying to sabotage my work, or have you gone nuts?"

"Are those the only options? Besides, it's a controversial matter who might be sabotaging whom."

His mind fashions images of denial, punishment: she's naked but for a Rolex chastity belt; she's lounging in front of him, draping herself on pieces of furniture and such. The watch is first about her slender waist; then the stretchy band expands as she pulls it down over her hips, then to her ankles. She steps out of it, then slides it up one leg, up her thigh, like a garter. Finally it's somehow between her thighs, its much expanded band encompassing her from there to her shoulder. And everywhere he tries to touch is blocked by the face of the watch: its disc obscuring navel, nipple, nape of neck, then every orifice in turn. She keeps making it go round like reeling in a line, a rope; no, some irregular conveyer belt. The motion of rotation is smooth, does not seem to be abrasive to her body, perhaps even a stimulant? He spreads her thighs to find the hard circle shielding her softest parts; won't she accommodate him somewhere?

He rotates her to find any entry; her motion is faster than his. When he goes to probe with flesh of fingertip, anticipating delicate yielding tissue, he confronts instead the glass and metal disc, whose inner hands might as well point, instead of to numbers, to letters whose sum would spell NOLI ME TANGERE. The band's motion is smooth but her words abrasive, humiliating, as she continually eludes with the piece of magic hardware. "Hey, Sebastian, here's a riddle for you. What does a Rolex watch have in common with hemorrhoids? Every asshole eventually gets one!" He shudders, snaps himself out of it; as one can, with effort, do, to escape from a bad dream, working one's way in stages, toward hypnopompic state until finally, fully awake.

He's got to clear his head. He will leave her undisturbed a while, as she wishes. She's already gone off somewhere. To be still is all he requires. And quiet. Where can he satisfy these simple requirements? Surely there is an unoccupied room somewhere on these upper floors. He begins to walk, at his own pace. That alone feels liberating. He is drawn by light, finds its source, and enters a room whose sole occupants are blocks of wood, marble and sandstone; some clay. The floor has a dusting of tiny particles which reflect the sun to make the room awash with light; the skylight allows more still.

An oversized hardbound book of the work of Michelangelo lies face down on the floor—not a very respectful way to handle a book; binding will suffer. Curious that contemporary artists or aspiring artists study the ancient masters, yet their products bear not the least resemblance to the works of the latter. Sebastian's eyes now rest upon one of the larger objects in the room, covered by a dropcloth. He cannot finally resist satisfying his curiosity. In the nearly blinding light he gently tugs at the covering until it comes away, revealing a stunning secret: a twin of the gorgeous Georgetti sculpture that he has come, under Sarah's aegis, to identify with his very self.

Not an original work, of course—the perpetual quest for originality likely counterproductive, he believes—but undisputably beautiful. Were he to write, he would have coherence as his sole priority: the making of coherent form. He would gladly trade originality—that quality synonymous with calling attention to oneself or one's product—for elegant clarity. This piece before him, in any case, has a grandeur, and he finds it refreshing to feel flattered by one of Sarah's "tributes." To think that she does equate them: this sculpted form and his physique; idealized masculinity, strong yet graceful muscularity to his own form which seems to him, without Sarah's eyes, a shrunken-chested specimen. He recalls her whispering in his ear, before the start of the tour at the Catacombs, "Did you pose for that or what?"

He should tell her how flattered he is by her tribute; she would be pleased to receive from him an uncritical expression. "Sarah, do come here." The sculpture by his fellow Brit, Gill, though, continues to haunt him: stone Sebastian, whose calves seem to merge with the stone, like Ovid; whose arms are clasped above his head in seeming sexual submission; whose face has the repose of a Buddha's; whose stone-made-flesh has a certain voluptuousness.

"Opening my mail, I see?" She's annoyed; he forgot that he shouldn't disturb her, her work. Should he try to apologize? Explain?

"Could you perhaps indulge the excesses of a confessed self-reflexive voyeur?"

"Never give you a surprise party, Sebastian. And for goodness sake, wear a mask; this dust is bad for you." She finds a package in the corner, opens it and places a white oval paper muzzle over his nose and mouth, squeezes a clip over the bridge of his nose and pulls a blue elastic band tight to secure the thing. "Now you can be an alien too."

"Redundant, I'm afraid. But Sarah, I must tell you, this is beautiful, what you've made. It's absolutely . . . art." She looks disappointed.

"From the expert, huh? It's just a study, really. Like an exercise. Nothing original."

"Yes, I assumed those would be your sentiments."

"I guess I'm an open book."

"Hardly that. Do you know what I'd really like, Sarah?"

"I really don't have much time to chat now, Sebastian."

"To make love, right here, now, in this room."

"With your graven image?"

"With you. I want you so very much."

"Oh, Sebastian, please . . ."

"Oh Sarah please—let me—let me give you pleasure."

He's never known her to put any priority above their sexuality. She won't refuse him.

"I'm very confused." She does look unsure, vulnerable. Almost childlike, her finger in her mouth. Instead of his.

"That is an unusual sentiment indeed from my confident copperhead. Undauntable jaguar."

"I am human, Sebastian."

"I, too."

"That's part of it."

"Of what?"

"Of my confusion."

"Perhaps you could explain."

"Well first of all, I still don't really know why you're here. If you came to check up on me or what. I still don't know what the deal is with this business trip you're not on. And I guess you may as well know—I'm not sure how to say it—"

"Yes?" Her tone makes him anxious. The suspense is excruciating.

"I was thinking—"

"You were thinking—"

"That maybe we should be apart for a while." In his silence she continues. "Because I was all geared up one way, with you supposed to be away and me here with all my projects and now—now I'm just confused."

"We've come full circle then. Back to confusion."

"I can tell you feel hurt, C.B. Please don't be."

"How could I be otherwise? I am being punished for coming here to be with you, and for failing to take a business trip. May I be, then, your partner in confusion, if in no other respect?"

"You're getting all offended, Sebastian. Let me try explaining better, O.K.? Remember when you asked me before if I thought I would ever exhaust the martyr material?"

"I guess I feared you would finish me off one way or the other, Sarah. If you'll forgive me, I feel like a horse about to be sent off to the glue factory. A less noble end than the drama of your art might have provided."

"But that's just what I mean. I've been examining that—what you always want me to do with my ideas; I thought you'd approve of that at least. I know I have a tendency to get carried away, creatively. I mix up my life with my art; I can't help it. It's the way I make sense of things, the way I make sense of the world. At least try to. It's hard to explain to someone who's not an artist, because there's a special relationship to imagination that's incredibly intense."

He knew he should have disclosed to her his writerly ambitions.

"The thing is, I suddenly realized where all this could go. Just today I figured it out, that you were right, that your worries were valid, that I might abuse you somehow. Exploit, like you said. And I don't want my fiancé to be a prop in some performance art piece."

"That sounds like something I would say to you."

"I know. I know it does."

"Sarah, come back home with me. Let's forget everything that happened today, shall we? We could begin anew. I won't ever interrupt your work again, and I won't defile your studio with my presence any longer, but I implore you to accompany me to our bedroom, where we are sure to make sense of things."

"I'm not sure if forgetting is what we should do, Sebastian. I know at least I have to figure this out. On my own. I just need some time to think."

"Time to think, Sarah, that's the grand cliché, like 'not tonight, dear, I've a headache.' Surely a woman of such intense imagination could arrive at something more original than that. We do live together, after all. Unless you were contemplating moving out as well?"

"No, Sea, listen to me. You're all upset, and you're not really hearing me." She embraces him firmly, and whispers gently, into his ear, "S.O.S. from S.o'Z. to S.o'B."

"Will you come back with me then?" Sebastian wishes he had his volume of Aristotle with him. He would sit in the room and read, focus, reassure himself.

"I can't come now, but I promise I won't be too long. Just a few more hours to finish some pieces. Please, Sebastian. I need that from you. I need you to be alright."

"I came a very long way to get here, and I'm not certain of the way back. I don't have the Jag."

"That is unusual."

"Frankly, I feel a bit unsteady on my feet."

"In that case, I wouldn't recommend the stairs. Let me walk you over to the elevator."

"Oh yes, the one you called 'iffy.' There will be performance art before the day is through after all."

"No such thing. Now come with me." She takes his arm, clasping her hand in his after gingerly removing the mask, walking him out of the room and over to a rather sinister looking rectangle outlined in the wall. She presses a black button and he hears the sound of a motor. He peers in and sees a cage creeping toward him, watching its vertical progress makes him anxious indeed.

"Sarah, since you've embraced the practice of examining your ideas, would you do me the favor of evaluating this separation. Are you quite sure your resolve not to abuse me isn't in disguise—subconsciously, of course—simply a substitute abuse? Sending me away like this—"

"Sebastian, I'm not abandoning you. Repeat after me, Sarah is not abandoning Sebastian. There are tons of buses at the corner, getting back home is not complicated at all, and I promise you the elevator will get you back down. I've ridden it lots of times. I'll see you in a few hours, O.K., Sea Bass? You know how to ride it, I know you do."

At this point it would be humiliating as well as futile to persist, resist. Counterproductive if he wants, as he so desperately does, to sort things out with her. He must be patient. He will be brave. The noise of the contraption he is about to enter is not easy for him to categorize: part futuristic, part chthonic. The chamber's appearance feels entirely the latter as he holds his breath and steps in, first opening the metal grating that he must close upon himself—or she for him—in order to descend. If he lingers he will lose courage, and come closer still to losing her. It is she who helps him close the inner fence; beckons with index finger for him to bring his face forward so that she can kiss him through one of the large diamonds of the steel pattern.

"Sarah, you'll finish the wedding rings?"

"Of course, Sweet Bee, of course I will. That's one of the reasons I have to stay. A priority project. And don't mind this thing, it's a little spooky; that's all. Are you ready?"

A button is pressed; the steel flooring underneath him begins to descend. The wooden walls of his cage, though far apart, feel claustrophobic, and he presses his palms over his ears against the hideous creaking as the cables take him down. Paradoxically, he feels more enclosed than he would in a smaller passenger lift; that closeness would be comparatively comforting. To have it over is all he wants. He does not feel at all "in place." Sarah is intuitive; he must trust her; she promised it wouldn't break; he'd get down. At last it creaks to a halt, so he can release himself from his insecurity, pull aside the grating.

And yet, this release is incomplete, for Sebastian realizes that he has no wish at all to leave without her, to place himself again into the void. He journeyed far to find her, to talk with her, come to an understanding: learn. There is much yet to learn and understand, and he requires her assistance; at least her cooperation. Clearly, he must go back up. He'll plead with her to reconsider; is he not articulate? And if she'll but allow him, he knows he can convince her with means other than words. If they can but return to the bed from which he never should have risen today, there can assuredly be resolution.

He must convince himself, however, before he can convince her; that is, rally himself with optimistic sentiments such as these, for stepping back into the horrid box is anything but reassuring. He sweeps to the side the lozenge-patterned grating, hesitates a moment before slamming it shut, fencing himself in. This eerie chamber, with its bleak illumination from a single bulb in its crude ceiling; this is the chamber which will convey him upward, as close as he can come to flight.

He presses the button. The beast of speed and motion which he has allowed swallow him begins to rise, accompanied by irregular creaking noises. Yes, he will convince her to forget, as well as forgive. He will elicit the playful in his sweet fiancée. How can I refuse you, she will say, when you take such risk to get to me? My Silly Boy, my Sugar Bear, my Secret Solo-Ball.

The sound of the machine's gears occurs in increments now; he should be nearly there—three flights, four. Why does he think of Sarah's stories of Jewish ritual, recited each night for forty-nine days. Was it forty-nine? Nursery rhymes she finally consented to have translated. "Who knows one? I know one. One is the Eternal. Who knows two? Who knows three?" Would he could know how long this suffering would last, that he might count it off; like marking little boxes housing numbers, on a calendar: this many days until sanity. Mete out one's endurance. Or would he could know how to make it—suffering—cease. The sound stops. The cage has stopped moving. How can it when they're not yet there; not quite. It appears to be between floors; all the thing needs is to add a few more increments. Is there no alarm button? Unlikely to work, if there were. What can he do to make the cage move?

"Sarah," he shouts, "Sarah!" Who could hear? Could she, with her practiced intuition, not sense his distress? Though if she has temporarily severed her psyche from his, from thoughts of him— All he requires is to get to that top floor, to the statue: most masculine of all representations of the saint, and perhaps even more so than the Georgetti itself, if possible. Sarah would not shun her own handiwork, would she? Might she this moment be gazing at the effigy of himself, perhaps stroking herself, doubting, even momentarily, the wisdom of her move away from him. Her body will want to come toward him again, not be separate. As soon as they parted she would have to have questioned—oh this horrid fence as if he were some caged creature.

He could try to force his body through one of the diamond-shaped apertures, to get to the floor below, as it seems the between here is not quite halfway: nearer to what's below than what's above, alas. But if he missed, he'd go straight down the shaft; that makes him shudder. No, up is the only possible way.

All the way up to the roof if he could; because there's something he wants to proclaim from the rooftops, to tell those below; perhaps even write in the sky with the letters one sometimes sees which appear to be made of cloud. First, of course, he needs surmount the obstacle before him. Surely having overcome many today; or rather survived; having already survived, as many as any one person could bear, is it not logical, likely even, that he'll clear the last hurdle, having, as it were, amassed, albeit sluggish, momentum?

"Oh Sarah, please come to the freight elevator at once—an emergency!" Were she present, it would be nothing at all like this. She'd make it erotic, a game, as she can transform even a ride through a carwash, give it mythic dimensions. This chthonic journey only Eros could redeem. How foolish he must appear—to no observer—with his head sticking out of a lozenge like some ludicrous guillotine. How he appears, however, is not, for once, priority, as he is overwhelmed with feeling, a much larger mass of feeling.

* * *

And a most uncomfortable one that Sebastian is presently experiencing: of constriction, of pressure, "stuck-ness"; quite the opposite of his favorite feeling, of entering her: enclosure, embrace, when he knows that together they will work toward perfect accommodation, where the physics of expansion and contraction take on mystical dimensions.

That's the nearest thing Sebastian knows in his adult life to transcendent experience: what is revealed in the orders of flesh. He'll stand by that, given the chance. One more chance? Sebastian, who has felt the difficulty, the impermeability of too many barriers in his life, feels this is one instance—happily repeated —in which a door opens to him naturally, gracefully, joyfully. Hasn't she often said, when he must finally slip away, spent, limp, "Sebastian, it's the woman who's supposed to sigh." He rather likes her teasing, when it's that sort.

If only he could transform this constriction into that liberation; would involve a reconstituting, an alchemy he has no training in. Willpower would not suffice, cognitive forces grossly inadequate. Moreover, he's making it worse for himself, knows he is, because he can't any longer apply his mind to the task at hand, simply overwhelmed. What was the task? Something requiring a miracle of the magnitude he no longer believes is possible, not for himself. He recalls the oft-quoted phrase, "harder to enter than for a camel to pass through the eye of a needle." All kingdoms closed to him now. He envisions, unbidden, a sandy-colored animal licking the narrow metal instrument's eye, like a lollipop, or diminutive hoop held by some cruel and cunning circus master.

Then he is thinking, now why a camel? Why not a dog or an elephant? Well, of course, it's historical context, he knows that, but he feels perversely opaque, as if his mind's just shut off, simply refuses to attend. More than occasionally and always when he most needs, it does; deliberately distracts him with what Sarah calls "dreck." Perhaps if he were a writer, rather than one who sometimes writes, or means to write, all this debris would not accumulate.

A bad pun assaults him: one hump or two? Her song in Hebrew, was it called Hagadah? "'Only one kid, only one kid. My father bought for two zuzim.' Don't make me translate, Sebastian; it won't make sense to you." He recalls she recalled only fragments. "And a cat came and ate. . . ." He jumps to elephants, with larger or little ears—size of his own member—might as well try to bring it along as well—no doubt would not get through —disqualified. The whole apparatus retracts, not just the tender twin appendage. He has previously reflected—now again the fear, that his private vehicle to the sublime is what binds him most to earth. He shivers to think of her quoting from Donne. Compasses. Orgasms. Death.

He sees the slender needle's eye going over the camel's hump like a rigid lasso. Is it slightly expanding or is the hump shrinking? Perhaps the implement is not really a needle, is in fact a rope that once fastened will be pulled tighter, cut off circulation, take away once and forever— Oh, what is the use? The thing is stuck. Stuck round the pinnacle of a protuberance and destined to remain so, never expanding enough to surround the breadth of the base, and thus a perpetual reminder of a thwarted, nay failed struggle: some pathetic badge, far worse than wearing half a suit.

He hears Sarah's voice in his head, the tender way she sometimes, when he least expects it, says, "I think you're too hard on yourself." Is he that? Or is it the world that is hard and he too soft, as it presses upon, against, him? He bruises instead of adapts or accommodates; not softening, moistening, ripening—what he could learn from a world of women. Instead he grows brittle, dents too easily. Then when he attempts to apply pressure back, he dents just the same. This process, in any case, may take a very long time, and a kind that can't be measured. No matter, he'll never get that watch back now. If it isn't in the mobile it's surely in some other—sculpture. He fears he will never see Sarah again.

She'll hate him, condemn him, feel betrayed; now when he needs her more than ever—love is like a policeman: never available when one's vulnerable. Now he's in need he could search and search; call with his voice till he has no voice left, all in vain.

Perhaps he is being punished somehow, and not just by Sarah, for how can something this ontologically dire be dismissed or written off as mere bad luck? To lose his only solace—grand finale to an ill fated, colossally frustrating day? If he hadn't procrastinated on the wedding; if he'd appreciated her more, perhaps he wouldn't be in danger of losing—if he had been less pedantic, less pretentious, less needy, more? Too clinging, not enough; too dismissive; less, or more, insecure? "They flee from me that sometime did me seek—" The silver Jaguar hood ornament, brilliant in sunlight, might fly away, no longer caring to distinguish this particular vehicle. And she—the poet Thomas Wyatt—Sarah are you familiar?—the very great sixteenth century poet, Sir Thomas Wyatt? A jaguar for an hind. He should have at least hinted of his wish to be a writer; tried to explain his interpretation of Aristotle. He could so easily have shared the fragment he showed to the Padre. Eros hundred-arrowed.

If he reached the roof, he could bask in the light of the sculpture studio. He could quietly observe, wouldn't bother her, not a peep. Just to be up there with her, even near. Then he would flip a coin, and watch it flutter, brilliant, metallic, so near to the sky; open the skylight and let it escape. He would be cautious lest it gather momentum and become inadvertent projectile, through physics, and injure some innocent passerby far below. Though if he spotted an enemy, he'd release it glibly, gladly. But the coin would be more a diversion, seduction, a way to gain someone's attention, so that he might call to that person, as loud and as clearly as possible, even thus weakened, and from this great distance.

"I beg your pardon, Sir or Madame, if you please," is what he'd say. One individual's ears would suffice. "I have an announcement to make; an announcement about the earth, the very earth upon which you stand. I can say with conviction, based upon my arrival here, and my forthcoming arrival at an altar—" On the other hand, he could be silent and simply make one reckless gesture, itself more powerful, more devastating a statement than any spoken words—

"Regarding this earth, I wish to say—are you still listening?—I wish to say it won't—although previously I could have sworn it would, if I did, if I said two simple words—I now however realize that, happily, it won't, because I will; that is, because I DO. INDEED I DO!" The person's face, from afar, appears puzzled, annoyed, then disgusted. "Do forgive me; I am not making myself clear. What I mean to say is that I wish to say, I DO, and that I WILL, and by some hitherto unperceived causal link, it won't; that is it won't because I WILL. It; that is, the earth, will not—well, it's only logical—do you follow?"

Surrender to words, or surrender from, to embrace the abyss? He would prefer it be the former, but fears, the latter. At times the hypothetical choice seems arbitrary; yet anything—either of these extremes, would be more tolerable than enduring this constriction, this darkness: to be stuck here, yearning for air, for light, the clouds, or stars.

Mary Caponegro is the winner of the 1988 General Electric Award for Younger Writers. Her short fiction has appeared in *Conjunctions, Fiction International, Sulfur, Mississippi Review, Tyuonyi,* and other periodicals. She has taught creative writing and literature at Brown University, the Rhode Island School of Design, and the Institute of American Indian Arts in Santa Fe, New Mexico. She currently resides in the Finger Lakes region of New York, where she is Assistant Professor of English at Hobart and William Smith Colleges.